D0502188

The Way
Past Winter

ALSO BY KIRAN MILLWOOD HARGRAVE:

The Girl of Ink & Stars

The Island at the End of Everything

The Way
Past Winter

KIRAN MILLWOOD HARGRAVE

chronicle books · san francisco

First published in the United States of America in 2020 by Chronicle Books LLC.
Originally published in the United Kingdom in 2018 by Chicken House Ltd.
Text copyright © 2018 by Kiran Millwood Hargrave.
Illustrations © 2020 by Lauren O'Hara.
Hand lettering © 2020 by Natalia O'Hara.

Library of Congress Cataloging-in-Publication Data available.

ISBN 978-1-4521-8155-4

Manufactured in China.

Design by Jennifer Tolo Pierce.
Typeset in Fairfield LH and Bookeyed Susan.

10 9 8 7 6 5 4 3 2 1

Chronicle Books LLC
680 Second Street
San Francisco, California 94107

Chronicle Books—we see things differently. Become part
of our community at www.chroniclekids.com.

For N̦ & my brother John, the brave ones

Before

*O*nce upon a time far distant from our own, in a place very near, there lived a bear named Eldbjørn. He was the child of two ancient spirits, born on the timeless island of Thule. He was brought here to this wood when the forest was seeds, and grew with it until he was old and mighty as an oak, and rooted just as deeply.

His den was beneath a vast birch that grew in the heart-center of the forest, cupped in its hollow trunk. All winter he slumbered, and his snores shook the icicles from the trees for miles around. In summer he woke and fed on the honey scooped from the combs of bees, and fish from the rushing river. He loved the sun, would stretch his claws out like a joyful cat and knead the baked Earth, basking in the warmth of her. For centuries he watched his forest blossom and freeze, the turning of seasons neat and right as the new moon.

But in the forest's thousandth year, men arrived. The first Eldbjørn knew of it was a shaking within the Earth. The running of a hundred foxes, the worrying of two hundred hares. Then the wolves came bounding, farther into the dense trees than ever before. Over his head, birds came flocking, turning startled wheels in the sky.

Eldbjørn knew it was an especially bad sign that the creatures of the underground, the land, and the sky were fleeing, for bad things come in threes. He lumbered his bulk through the scared animals, moving fast to find what they ran from. His heart broke at what he saw. Three larch trees felled. A square mile of moss ripped up, and mounted on wood:

A house.

It had sprouted at the boundary of the forest, built from the stolen homes of songbirds and snakes. He saw glinting axes, and sap-bleeding trees, and reindeer leashed to a sleigh, their haunches matted with blood from whips.

In his heart was sadness, and fear, and from these grew their dangerous cousin: anger. His swiped at the house and sent the thatch flying. He tore the men from its walls like honey from a hive, and threw them from his bounds. He unleased the reindeer, and they trembled by the sleigh, already unable to remember what freedom was.

But these settlers were just the start. More and more came, and though Eldbjørn raged and wept, there was nothing he could do to stop the humans from coming and cutting and building. Each passing year, he shrank a little more, his grief swallowing him whole. He kept closer and closer to his heart-tree. Finally, one day, when the humans' homes outnumbered the bear caves, Eldbjørn had become nothing more than a sad soul. Now he was just a spirit secreted inside his tree's trunk.

You might not be able to see him anymore, but Eldbjørn is the reason the forest stays alive. Men may live and die here, but Eldbjørn ensures the forest will survive forever, its guardian the pulse that ties it to life, even as men bring small deaths—

"And women?"

Mila started, jolted from the reverie of her mother's tale by her brother's interruption. They were warm beside the fire, their bodies pressed together in a line before Mama, who sat on the woven seat of the low chair

Papa had built her. The wooden beams of their home arched over her head like branches, and the whole room smelled of lingonberry stew and sap glue. Tucked as she was beneath her father's arm, Mila could imagine she was Eldbjørn, nestled in his beloved trunk, safe from the world. That was, until Oskar interrupted. He was seated on her other side, and beyond him was her sister Sanna.

"Oskar!" snapped Sanna, and Mila could tell she was rolling her eyes. She was only a year older than Oskar but acted like she was a grown woman. "Not everything is boys versus girls."

"Oh yes?"

"Yes. Because girls would win."

Mama smiled and arched her back, tilting her belly toward the licking flames. Mila thought she could see it ripple, imagined her brother or sister inside, nearly ready to come into the world. Mila couldn't wait to no longer be the youngest. But more than that, she couldn't wait to hear the end of Mama's story.

"Oskar's right," continued Mama, and Oskar preened. "And women. We are all of us guilty of making our mark on the forest."

"But women make things, not break them. We make homes out of the wood men destroy," said Sanna. Oscar shoved her and she shoved him in return, but Papa reached over Mila's head and pulled Oscar back by his collar, his garnet ring glinting in the firelight.

"What can we do?" said Mila, stricken. "Should we leave?"

"It is our right as much as the animals' to be here," said Papa. "Don't listen to your mama's story. That is all it is."

"Stories are just another way of telling the truth," said Mama, her dark eyes shining.

"So is that why you're having another baby?" said Mila, wide-eyed. "Because bad things come in threes?"

Mama laughed softly. "Perhaps, though I was thinking this story is mainly true because it reminds us that we must take care of our forest."

"I will," said Mila, feeling a fierceness alight in her belly. She rested her hand on Mama's and felt her sibling moving. "I will look after the trees as well as my little sister."

Oskar made a retching sound. "You're so soft, Mila."

Mila flushed, but Mama's warm hand enclosed hers, and she brought her head down as close as she could to Mila's ear, so only she could hear. "My Milenka," she whispered. "The softest of us all—and so the strongest."

Now

PART I

Home

CHAPTER ONE

The House in Eldbjørn Forest

It was a winter they would tell tales about. A winter that arrived so sudden and sharp it stuck birds to branches, and caught the rivers in such a frost their spray froze and scattered down like clouded crystals on the stilled water. A winter that came, and never left.

A whole year passed, then three, and still it stayed. People spoke of curses and offered up prayers and promises. They blamed mages, or their neighbors, or the jarls who ruled their villages and towns.

But blame didn't break the winter, and soon no one could remember warmth except from fire, or green apart from the silvery hue of the fir trees. Carts were abandoned in favor of sleighs, fine horses lost their worth until they were all traded for mountain ponies or mewling husky pups or other animals that knew snow. Bears sank into perpetual hibernation, wolves slunk into the shadows of the vast forest. Some folk moved from their frozen land, but most stayed, and, as people do, changed to fit their changed world.

They changed their stories, too. Gone were tellings of honey and plenty: Tales became warnings, sharp as bee stings. The fire-geese who bore the sun on their backs in summer became ice-swans who nip at exposed fingers and toes, snapping them clean off. The river nymphs became ice maidens who stalk the bottom of frozen lakes, waiting to pull wayward children under. Wistful voices spoke of magical islands where spring waited, of golden waterfalls streaming into pools of sunlight, but always these places were beyond reach, just past the frozen horizon.

In the winter's fifth year, its grip still tightening on the southern river towns and northern mountain cities, a whole new order of cold wove itself tight as a basket about the families that lived in the remotest parts of the land. And it was in a small house folded into a narrow pocket of forest rimed with snow window-high, that three sisters and their brother were having a disagreement over a cabbage.

"Please don't boil it again, Sanna," pleaded Pípa, the youngest. She sat shivering, her hands over her cold ears, lip curled as she regarded the shriveled, hard-leafed vegetable. "We have had nothing but boiled all week."

"I'll not be told what to do by a child not even old enough for her given name," said Sanna briskly, like a superstitious woman thrice her seventeen years might, for Pípa was seven. It would be another year before they could be sure the evil eye had passed over her, when she would be regifted with her true name. "And besides, it's the way to get the most good out."

She stood with her cutting knife hovering, looking for the best incision point for the particularly hard and meager cabbage.

"There's dripping," said Mila hopefully, trying not to echo her little sister's whine. "We could fry—"

"And use up firewood to get the dripping hot enough?" chided Oskar from his spot furthest from the fire. "We must boil it. Grow up, Pípa. I've had enough of your trembling lip."

"Leave her, Oskar," said Mila, wrapping her arm around Pípa and frowning at their big brother. He was nothing like he used to be before Papa left; he was becoming a stranger. Then, they could not get him to be silent. Now he spoke only to spit thanks at Sanna for the food she gave him each morning before he waded into the thigh-high snow to check his traps, or to tell one of his little sisters off.

Mila caught up Pípa's stiff fingers and blew her hot breath on them. "Come, Píp, let's not trouble Sanna—she knows her cabbages."

"That I do!" said Sanna, having located the cabbage's weakest point and bringing the knife down with a satisfying *thwack*. "Boiled it is."

Outside, one of the dogs started to bark. Mila knew it was Dusha—her voice was higher than her brother's, more whiny and insistent, like Pípa's. A moment later it was joined by Danya's whip-crack yowl.

"Those dogs!" huffed Sanna. "Oskar—"

But Mila was already on her feet, taking her fur-lined boots from beside the fire. "I'll go."

She threw on her russet cloak and wrapped her fox fur around her brown hair, but before she could unbolt the door, someone knocked twice, and then twice more, in a jaunty rhythm that had become familiar to the family over the past months.

"Wait!" called Sanna, but Mila grinned mischievously and drew the bolt. She heard her sister swear loudly and clatter the saucepans, searching for the copper one that they sometimes used as a mirror.

A mountain pony was tied to the mounting post in the yard and a boy stood before Mila. He was Sanna's age and Oskar's height, with a plump, handsome face, fair where all the Oreksons were dark. He flushed when he saw Mila's teasing smile.

"Back again, Geir?" said Mila. "I didn't think we'd sent any knives for sharpening this week."

"Just the one," said Geir as Mila heard Sanna skidding into place behind her. Mila looked up at her big sister from under her fox fur and waggled her eyebrows. Sanna had let her hair down and pinched her cheeks into a rosy flush. She'd even bitten her lips in an effort to redden them, and she'd broken the skin slightly on the lower one. She pulled Mila out of the way with a pincer grip.

"Hello, Geir." Sanna's voice was oddly husky, as if she had a cold.

"Hello, Sanna," squeaked Geir.

Mila snorted and stomped her way back to the kitchen, pulling the door closed behind her to keep the warmth in. They'd grown used to the pathetic exchanges that passed for conversation between their sister and the knife-sharpener from Stavgar.

Oskar looked up from where he was finishing slicing the cabbage with his hunting knife. Its handle was intricately carved to look like roots twisted across it, and it had a thick blade, better suited to cutting rope and wood than vegetables. "Geir again?"

"Yep," said Mila, removing her hat and rolling her eyes.

"Were they kissing?" giggled Pípa.

"Pípa!" scolded Oskar. "Don't be ridiculous." He looked at Mila, disgust clear on his face at the thought of their older sister kissing a boy. "They weren't, were they?"

Mila thought about teasing him, but then her stomach rumbled. She didn't have the energy. "Of course not. He's just bringing a knife."

"Another one?"

"Mmm." She collapsed on the bench beside the fire, watching the steam rising from the water that would soon be the same thin grayish cabbage soup they'd eaten for weeks now.

Mila listened to the knife ripping through the cabbage and strained to hear the murmurs of Sanna and

Geir's exchange. The lovely bell of Sanna's laugh, so like Mama's, rang out before the front door closed with a creak and a bang, blowing the kitchen door open and sending cold fingers of wind raking across Mila's cheeks. Sanna floated in, a faraway look on her thin face as she gazed at something in her palm.

"What's that?" asked Pípa.

"Nothing," said Sanna hurriedly, pinning the something, gleaming, onto her cloak. "A gift." It was a brooch, intricately worked from elk horn, full of pale swirls that recalled a foaming sea. It was very fine.

"And what did you give in return?" asked Mila, bringing vivid spots of red to her sister's cheeks.

"Nothing," said Sanna briskly, brandishing the newly sharpened knife mock-threateningly at Mila. "A gift shouldn't be given with the expectation of something in return."

"That's the fourth time he's been round in a week," said Oskar.

"Hmm," said Sanna, purse-lipped.

"It's a long way from Stavgar—he'll be riding back in the dark."

"Hmm."

"Perhaps next time you could invite him in for dinner?"

Mila saw a look pass between her older siblings, full of something she didn't understand.

"Yes," said Sanna. "Maybe I will." She swallowed, then said in a firm tone that meant the subject was closed, "Now please tell me you're done butchering that cabbage."

—⟫⟫⟫—

The dim day fell into the dark lap of dusk, and the small house filled with the smell of boiled cabbage soup that meant dinner was ready. Sanna was just about to ladle Pípa's portion into her chipped wooden bowl when Dusha set about barking, followed by Danya.

"Not Geir again?" said Oskar, and Sanna shook her head.

"Probably just spooked. I'll go and calm them," said Mila, in no hurry for her bowl of soup. She put on her cloak and hat for the second time, opened the door a crack, and stepped into the snow, which glowed a silvery gray in the uncertain light.

"Coming, Dush-Dush! Coming, Danya!"

Keeping her head bowed against the biting wind, she heaved the door closed behind her and began to trudge through the drifts toward the dog shed with its wooden gate, hands tucked under her armpits to keep them warm. But she had not taken more than three steps before she collided with something.

"*Javoyt!*" Mila stumbled back, stepped on her cloak, and nearly fell. She regained her balance and looked up. Her heart thudded almost as loud as the wind. Now she knew why the dogs were barking.

CHAPTER TWO

The Stranger

"Man's language from such a little girl," said a voice, deep and punchy as Danya's barks, which grew louder. "What is your name?"

Mila pulled her scarf up to cover her lips, swallowing down a fearful tang as she smelled a horrifying animal scent, bitter as rotten leaves. Before her stood a horse, as square and as huge, it seemed to her, as a barn. On its back sat a man so swathed in fur he looked as large as the horse itself, a beast on a beast. A woodcutter's axe like her father's glinted at his waist, and his eyes flashed gold and wild above shadowy stubble.

Behind him were a dozen smaller figures on ponies, cloaked and hooded and bearing torches. One of them carried a pennant, embroidered, Mila saw, with a bear beneath a tree. The tree's roots, elaborately tangled, glinted with gold as the pennant flickered in the wind.

From all of them there lifted a steam of heat, and the ponies were snorting and stamping, shying away from the dogs, who were throwing themselves at the gate. The man raised a hand, and both dogs fell silent, collapsing on the ground like emptied sails.

"No!" Mila wrenched her feet from where they seemed frozen in the snow. "Dush! Dan—"

But the dogs were only lying quietly, noses resting on their forepaws, eyebrows twitching above wide-open eyes. Even the trees behind them seemed to still.

Mila turned cautiously back to the assembled company. She peered past the man at the next rider. His chin was unstubbled, as if he were a boy of Oskar's age. Perhaps he was this man's son? She looked into the next face, then the next. All the riders were boys, some perhaps only a year older than she. Surely one man could not have so many sons?

Her voice was caught in her throat, fluttering like a captured bird. The man swung his huge leg over the back of the horse and landed in the snow. No, that wasn't quite right. . . .

Mila stared at the man's feet. He wore fine, unscuffed black leather boots that showed no signs of a hard journey, but that was not what made her stare.

The man had not landed in the snow—he had landed *on* it. He hadn't sunk into the soft powder, even though she could feel it seeping over the tops of her boots, and his companions' ponies were in almost to their hocks.

Mila dragged her head up and saw he was looking directly at her, with those fierce eyes. When Mila again looked down, he was up to his calves in snow. What's more, the tops of his fine boots were now tied about his calves with lengths of golden cord, like the tree roots on the pennant.

Mila blinked, and the man smiled, baring teeth gray and slabbed as charred wood. She swallowed, bitterness rising like a tide beneath her tongue.

"Winter-well-met," said the man, pausing for her to return the greeting, which she did not. "Aren't you going to welcome us?"

"I . . ." Mila cleared her throat and tried again. "I do not know you."

The man gave a laugh as clipped as his voice. "And I do not know you, child. But where I am from, we always welcome a visitor who comes, tired, to our door."

"Mila?"

She spun around. She had not heard the door open, but now Oskar, without a cloak or a fur, his boots unlaced, was pulling it shut behind him. Beyond him, Mila saw the distorted faces of her sisters pressed against the ice-filled window like twin moons.

"Mila, is it?" murmured the man. Mila felt a tightening behind her eyes, like the beginnings of a headache. She wished Oskar had not said her name.

Her brother approached as he might a circling wolf, wading carefully through the snowdrifts and placing himself between Mila and the man. He pushed her back slightly, and she knew he wanted her to go inside, but she did not want to leave him alone with them. His slight frame and bare head only made the man's bulk seem more overwhelming: a sapling set before an ancient oak.

"Who are you?" said Oskar, his back straight, his voice louder than it needed to be. Mila noticed that the wind seemed to have quietened, and though the trees were unnaturally still, Oskar's dark hair was blowing about his ears.

"I would speak to the man of the house," said the man, his golden gaze set over Oskar's head.

"I am he," said Oskar.

"Really? Where is your father?"

Mila felt a lump rise in her throat, and heard the same tightness in Oskar's voice as he replied, "Gone."

"How old are you?"

"Sixteen years of winter."

"And your name?"

"Oskar."

"Oskar," repeated the man, a cruel smile playing about his stubbled cheeks. "Winter-well-met, Oskar. As I was about to tell Mila"—the tightness behind her eyes ratcheted up—"we are come from the south. We've been trading."

"Trading what?"

"Treasure." The man grinned and clicked his fingers. His companions pulled their cloaks up so the golden cord about their ankles was more clearly revealed. Mila had never seen gold worked in such a way, spun into thin, flexible strands. But the result was not exactly beautiful. It was knotted and rough-looking, like the roots carved on Oskar's knife. Ugly and fine at once, like the stranger.

Oskar took a wondering step toward them, and as one, the boys dropped their cloaks again. "Where are you taking such riches?"

"North." A look at the man's face told Mila that Oskar would not be getting more information than that, but she knew there was not much north: only the mountain city of Bovnik and the Boreal Sea, with its stories of magical islands where spring still lived.

"What business have you in Bovnik?" asked Oskar.

"Our own," sneered the man, his voice harsher than before. "In the meantime, we hope for food, and permission to start a fire and pass the night."

After a moment's hesitation, Oskar replied, "I am not sure we can give it."

The man took a step forward, and Mila's heart swelled with pride as Oskar gave only the smallest of flinches.

"What did you say, boy?"

"Winter is falling harder lately," said Oskar. "And the forest is less giving by the day—"

"We are well aware, having ridden through its heart," spat the man. "And perhaps it is only that the forest has given enough."

Oskar swallowed, then continued, "We have no food to spare. I cannot risk my family."

"Ah. So there are more of you?"

A stab of foreboding pierced Mila's chest. *Do not answer him,* she willed Oskar. The man flicked his gaze to her for a moment, almost as if he'd heard her. But Oskar, seeming to think the man was softening, plunged on.

"Yes. Sanna, Pípa, and Mila. I have three sisters."

"Three? What a curse." The others laughed, and Mila bristled as Oskar joined in half-heartedly. "But such pretty names."

Oskar's face was suddenly fearful. "So, you see, I cannot risk running short of food."

"So, I do see," crooned the man. "But surely you can begrudge us some ground, some dry moss to start our fire?"

"Of course," said Oskar. "I'll return with the moss." He squared his shoulders as he turned back toward his sister. "Come, Mila."

"Goodnight, Mila," called the man.

The pain spiked her temples once more as she stepped over the threshold and Oskar closed the door behind them. Mila released the breath she had been holding and shuddered. She knew she would not sleep well with such wildness so near.

"What happened?" Pípa blurted. Oskar was shivering, and Sanna knelt to take off his boots. "Who were they?"

But Oskar only waved Sanna away and drew Mila to him, rubbing her shoulders before sweeping her into a tight hug. "Are you all right, Milenka?"

Mila leaned into her big brother. It had been so long since he had called her that, or held any of them. Since Papa had walked into the white, five winter years before, Oskar had grown up so fast it seemed he had left loving them behind, just as Papa had.

"Yes," she murmured.

Oskar gave her a final squeeze and released her. "Good. Now, none of you speak to them, all right? I'll share some moss, and then we stay inside until they are gone. None of you go out tomorrow until I say so. Agreed?"

Even Sanna, who hated taking orders from her younger brother, nodded. Mila turned her head to the iced window, and fancied she saw a shadow twitch away. The man had not told them his name. He had her brother's and sisters' names, though. He had hers.

CHAPTER THREE

A Face at the Ice Window

Many hours later, something woke Mila, bringing her up from a deep sleep, gasping. She lay still as her heartbeat slowed, listening to the sounds of her sleeping family. She liked this about living in constant winter: They all slept in the kitchen together, on pallets by the fire for warmth. Sanna, who had been twelve when the winter began, spoke longingly of how she'd once had her own bedroom for summer, with cotton curtains, but now the door to the summer rooms, with their thinner walls and larger windows, was boarded up. Besides, Mila could not imagine sleeping alone. Even before the winter, she'd sneak into Mama and Papa's bed and lie between them like a baby bird in its nest.

Pípa's light snuffles were close to her ear, and Sanna's deep sighing breaths were on her other side, her wing of raven-blue-black hair encroaching as always onto her straw pillow. But from the other side of her big sister, Oskar's shallow breaths were missing.

Mila sat up carefully, the heavy furs sliding off. Instantly she was cold, though she was stitched tight into her new winter vest, restuffed with moss by Sanna only last week. Even this close to the fire, her breath made little puffs, like a dragon from one of Mama's stories. Papa had especially liked those ones.

Papa. Mila breathed the word to herself, for the first time in months. There was a sort of unspoken rule between them that they did not talk about him, though he was everywhere in the house, from the trousers Oskar had recently grown into to his woodcutter's axes lying beside the fire, handles smooth with use.

But the stranger asking about his whereabouts had brought memories rushing back. She remembered so much about their father it was painful. He'd smelled of sap and woodsmoke. His eyes were ice-blue chips, like Sanna's. He'd had a wild laugh and a wilder heart, but it was kind, too. Not even her papa had been wild in the way that man outside was.

Allowing herself to think about Papa made Mila felt empty, like a hand that is dropped when it is used to being held, and, for the first time in ages, she wanted to do things that brought him closer, rather than pushing him further away. Maybe tomorrow, when the stranger and his boys had gone, they could go to the heart-tree, and sit and tell stories, like they used to.

She thought of the bear stitched on the man's pennant. Mama had told stories about Bjørn, the bear spirit who protects trees, and Eld, the lonely bear who fell in love with the sun. Most of all, though, she spoke of their son, Eldbjørn, and his ruined forest. Sad, lovely stories, nothing like the stranger.

Mila looked toward the dark ice window and had to clap a hand to her mouth to keep from screaming. A face, distorted and huge, was at the window. It was illuminated grotesquely by the fire, which made it broad and beastly, stretched as though it had no solid edges. Gold eyes glinted in the flickering light. And standing before the window—

"Oskar?" Mila whispered.

The stranger's face disappeared, and Oskar turned from where he had stood looking out. Mila slipped out of bed and went to him, bare feet cringing at the fierce cold of the floor where the rushes had grown thin. She stopped just short of touching him. Their hug seemed a lifetime ago; now distance stretched between them. His face was drained of blood, his eyes large and glassy.

"Oskar, what are you doing?"

"I was watching the men." Oskar's voice was quiet, harsh.

"What are they doing?"

"Nothing."

Mila craned to see past him. "You were talking to him."

"No, I wasn't." Oskar shifted to block her view. There was a sheen of sweat on his upper lip. He looked feverish.

"Do you need some broth? Shall I wake Sanna?"

"No," he said, barely containing his anger. "Go back to bed."

Mila jutted her chin and narrowed her eyes at him. "What's going on?"

A shadow, like an eel flickering under the surface of a lake, shifted in her brother's face. He looked suddenly older. He looked . . . not himself.

Mila reached up to touch the strange bulge of her brother's cheek, but he grasped her wrist in a rough grip, fingers cold on her bed-warm skin. She gasped and tears started in her eyes at the sudden hurt of it. He leaned closer. "Go back to bed, Mila."

A stab of pain at her temple joined the ache in her wrist as he released her. Chest heaving, Mila did as she was told, sliding quickly between her sisters, and pulling the furs up over her head, trying to control her breathing. A small hand found hers, and she realized Pípa was awake too. She shuffled her covers until her little sister's wide eyes shone at her in the dark.

"What's wrong with Oskar?" whispered Pípa.

Mila only held a finger to her lips. She did not want their brother—or the stranger—to hear them.

CHAPTER FOUR

Gone

"*Up!*"

The furs were pulled roughly off Mila. She cried out, raising her fists to protect herself, but it was only Sanna.

"Get up, Mila. Come on." The light was the pale gray of morning, and her elder sister was wearing her work dress, Geir's brooch pinned over her heart, her black hair pulled back into a severe bun. Her eyes were narrowed, her jaw tense with irritation.

"What's—?" started Pípa blearily, her hand still wrapped around Mila's fingers.

"The men are gone," said Sanna sharply.

"That's good," said Mila, shivering and attempting to pull the covers back over herself.

Sanna let out a brief, bitter laugh. "And so is our brother."

Mila felt an icicle of fear stab her chest.

"Oskar is gone?" squeaked Pípa.

Mila rubbed her eyes, trying to make her brain wake up faster. "Perhaps he followed them to the Stavgar boundary to see that they really left? Or to the heart-tree—"

Sanna looked at her sharply. "Why would he go there?"

"That man," started Mila, hesitantly. "Yesterday he asked where our father was, and . . . it made me think of Papa. Maybe Oskar went there because it made him think about him too."

"Oskar told us not to go there," said Pípa seriously.

"You know he doesn't listen to anyone's advice, not even his own," said Mila. "Or maybe he went to check the traps early?"

Sanna rolled her eyes, and the icicle in Mila's chest melted slightly into a trickle of annoyance. Why was Sanna not more worried?

"Should we go and check?" Mila said, bracing herself against the morning chill and hurrying over to the fire, where her tunic hung. She slid it over her head and wove her belt around her waist three times, knotting it at the side before pulling on her wool leggings. They were warm and smoky, and she took a deep breath, calming herself. "I can take Dusha and the sleigh—"

Sanna let out another strange, hiccuping laugh. Mila rounded on her. "What's so funny?"

"It's not funny at all," said Sanna, taking a deep breath and setting her shoulders square. *She looks very beautiful,* Mila thought through her anger, *and very distant.* "But we should have seen it coming."

"Seen what coming?" said Pípa.

"Another person leaving us," muttered Sanna, so only Mila, standing closest to her, could hear. "I'm always the one left behind."

Mila narrowed her eyes. "Oskar hasn't left."

Sanna looked as though she was going to say something in reply, but then she just swung around and took the snow bucket from its hook beside the fire.

"I'm going for fresh snow. You lay new rushes down— they're getting patchy in here."

"What should we have seen coming?" asked Pípa again, but Mila only shook her head. Mention of the rushes had brought back the memory of her bare feet on the freezing dirt floor, her strange exchange with Oskar.

"I saw something last night!" said Mila. "I've just remembered. Oskar was standing by the window. He was talking to someone outside, I think—"

Sanna stiffened, and on her face was a look Mila had no name for. "The ice is inches thick. You can't hear through it."

"Well, he was watching someone, then. And they were watching him back."

Sanna narrowed her eyes. "Go and get the rushes."

"Can't I look for him? He looked strange, like—"

"It sounds like a dream to me," said her sister sharply. "Do as I say."

She flung her shawl over her head and left the kitchen. A moment later they heard the wind howl, and a gust of winter air puffed through the kitchen, making the fire flicker, before Sanna closed the door behind her.

Mila knew that tone: As well as her laugh, Sanna's sternness was also Mama's. There was no point arguing. She opened the door to the store and reached up for the rushes where they hung drying on a hook. Her sleeves slid back and she saw a livid bruise around one wrist, purple and blue as a thundercloud. *It wasn't a dream*, she thought. There was a rustle behind her and she turned to see Pípa, still in her nightclothes, fur slippers on her feet.

"Come, Píp. Get dressed, and then you can help me lay the floor."

Sanna swept in with the fresh snow as they left the store, and was too slow wiping her eyes.

"Why are you crying?" said Pípa.

Sanna grimaced. "I'm not." She slammed the door behind her. Her pale cheeks were flushed with cold, her huge eyes stark. "Stop *staring* at me, Pípa."

"Were there tracks? Did you see which way—?" started Mila, but Sanna shook her head.

"Only an animal's," she said curtly. "Otherwise it's snow-smooth. Like they were never here at all."

She stomped to the kitchen to hang the bucket over the fire to melt. Mila went to the front door and opened it a small crack. Sanna hadn't lied—the yard was unblemished, aside from Sanna's dragging tracks looping from the door to where she'd fetched clean snow, and there were chopping-block-sized imprints, too big to be an elk or a wolf, circling the boundary, disappearing around the side of the house and out of Mila's sight. *North.*

"All gone?" asked Pípa, trying to peer past her.

Mila nodded, swallowing hard. She couldn't understand why Sanna wouldn't let her go and see where

Oskar was. Pípa leaned into her waist. "Can I put on my day clothes later? When Oskar comes back?"

Mila nodded. "We'll start with the food store. We can do the kitchen after breakfast, when . . . when he's home."

But even after they had relaid the rushes in the food store, the kitchen and the corridor, Oskar had not returned.

"He'll have gone straight to the traps," said Mila, more to comfort herself than Pípa.

"Without breakfast?"

"The boundary, then—"

"Without Danya?" interrupted Sanna tersely. "He never goes into the forest without that dog. He went with *them*."

Mila wanted to shake her. "What?"

"Isn't it obvious?" said Sanna, speaking as though to a small and stupid child. "He went with him."

"The man from last night? Why would he do that? He wouldn't," said Mila, suddenly feeling very hot.

"Why not? Why not choose adventures over three sisters? Over—what did Oskar say that man called us?—a *curse*."

Bad things come in threes. The phrase rose in Mila's mind, unbidden.

"Oskar loves us," said Pípa, her lower lip wobbling. "He wouldn't go away."

Sanna laughed hollowly. "Oh, yes, Oskar loves us, just like Papa loved us, just like Mama—"

"They did love us!" cried Mila, feeling as though she'd been punched.

But Sanna's eyes were wild and bright. "Papa loved us so much he left us, walked out and never looked back. And now Oskar has done the same."

Mila's breath was coming in little stabs, like a stitch. They never talked about how Papa left, how he rose early on the anniversary of Mama's death and walked into the winter without a hat or a cloak. "You don't know that. Oskar says Papa loved us, only he loved Mama more. He couldn't live here without her—"

"She was already gone!" Sanna was on her feet, shouting now. Mila saw spit flying from her mouth, and threw an anxious glance at Pípa. Mama had died giving birth to her, and they were careful not to talk about it much. "He was following her, but she was already years dead. He preferred to leave his family in the hands of our fickle brother, who ran as soon as a better offer came along. And who's left behind to pick up the pieces? Me—"

The heat in Mila expanded, making her hands tingle and pulling her to her feet too. "He wouldn't leave. He must have been taken."

"Did you hear a struggle? Do you see a sign of the door being forced, blood in the snow?" Sanna said, breathing raggedly. "No. And you heard him talking to someone!"

"There was something wrong with that man who was leading them, something bad." Mila thought of his feet on the snow, the way he had silenced the dogs with a gesture. "Something dangerous."

"Perhaps where you saw danger, Oskar saw excitement," said Sanna, quieter now. She stood, her shoulders slumped, long neck dipped, and Mila could see her nails digging into her palms. "And I don't blame him. If I were a man, I'd leave too. I'd walk out that door and never come back."

Mila felt the breath knocked from her chest. Pípa ran forward to cling to Sanna's skirts. "Don't go, San."

Sanna pushed her away roughly and gave another mirthless laugh. "I won't." She looked up and her eyes were bright with tears. "I've nowhere *to* go."

She threw her cloak over her shoulders, and a moment later they heard the door slam and the dogs begin to bark. Mila knew she was going to sit with them in the dog shed. It was what any of them did when they were upset.

She felt as though the floor had turned to snow slush beneath her feet, and sat down hard on the bench. Pípa was crying quietly, and Mila pulled her onto her lap, rocking her gently.

"Is . . . she . . . leaving?" said Pípa, hiccuping.

"No, she's only gone to sulk with the dogs," said Mila, in the brightest voice she could manage. "Hear them whining with her?"

"So . . ." began Pípa. "You don't think Oskar left us? He's coming back?"

Mila pressed her face into Pípa's thick braid, thinking hard. "I'll go and look for him. It'll be fast with both dogs. I'll check the traps, the heart-tree. He might be hurt, or . . ." She swallowed. "I'll be back before full dark if I leave now."

"Can I come?"

"Absolutely not." She patted Pípa to signal she wanted to get up. "I had better tell Sanna I'm going."

Mila wrapped herself in her cloak and hat, and paused a moment before grabbing Sanna's, too—she'd almost rather let her freeze for her meanness. She gave Pípa another quick hug before heading to the dog shed.

It was a low turf-roofed structure, always warm, even in winter. In a rare memory of her mother, Mila remembered her teasing Papa: *You spoil those dogs. It's better built than our own home!* It was true, in part: All the gaps in the walls were plugged with straw for extra protection against the wind, and the roof was double-thickness. Mila took a deep breath as she entered, inhaling the warm biscuity smell of the dogs, so comforting even in her saddest moments.

Sanna was squeezed into a dark corner, Danya bundled across her lap, Dusha lying alongside. Mila felt her temper subside, seeing her big sister, normally so composed, crumpled like a pile of rags beneath the dogs.

"I'm going to the heart-tree, and to check the traps."

"What's the use?" said Sanna, voice thick, as she extricated her hand from beneath Danya's chin. The dog gave a whining complaint, twitching his muzzle at her.

"He's gone, Mila. Just like Papa." She drew something out from the deer-hide pouch on her day belt. "I found this in the doorway when I fetched the snow."

In her palm lay their father's ring: dull bronze set with a large garnet, smoky and smooth from years of constant wear. Mila took it, scarcely breathing.

Their mother had given him that stone, quarried from the mine where she'd worked in Bovnik when he'd asked her to handfasten with him. In a clear, shining moment of memory, Mila remembered her father twisting the ring after lighting the wick in a dish of cold deer fat on the anniversary of their mother's death. *To bring her memory into the light.*

An awful sadness enveloped her worry for Oskar, like a heavy net closing over a shoal of panicking fish. *Papa.* His broad, bearded face, thumb working at the garnet, rubbing it to a shine, his ice-blue eyes desperate . . .

And the next day, he was gone. Oskar had called for his sisters and gone rushing into the snow-hushed forest, come back almost a day later, scratched to pieces and crying, the ring clenched in his hand. *He's gone. He's gone.* When he'd calmed, he told them how he'd scoured the forest.

I found this by the heart-tree, he'd finished, opening his palm to show the ring, which had left grooves in his skin.

Did you look in the tree? Are you sure Papa didn't just climb it? asked Mila. *Maybe he went to remember Mama.*

Oskar had fixed her with a look so haunted she'd paled in terror.

What is it?

He wasn't there. And we can never go back to the heart-tree, he'd said, in a voice as deadened as his eyes. *Promise me.*

They'd all promised. And as though to keep them caught in the awful memory of that day, the winter stretched and stretched. It was like Papa had taken spring with him, had left them in the cold.

"Mila?"

Mila felt a dread start to fill her throat as she looked from Sanna's face—the same high cheekbones, the same eyes as Papa's—to the ring and back again. She drew back, shaking her head. "Oskar wouldn't leave it behind. Perhaps he was struggling with them. Perhaps it fell off his finger—"

Sanna gave a sad smile. "It was in the center of the doorway, Mila. Placed there, for us to find. It's a message."

Mila shook her head even harder, setting the ear-flaps of her hat dancing. But even as she did so, the first seed of doubt planted itself in the pit of her stomach. She pushed it down, covering it over, making her voice strong and certain.

"I'm going to the heart-tree." She held out the ring and Sanna's hat and cloak. "I'm taking the dogs, so you'll need these to keep warm out here."

Sanna sighed, and slid the ring back into the pouch on her belt. She gently pushed Danya off her and stood up, reaching for her cloak. "I'm coming with you."

"What about Pípa?"

Sanna hesitated for a moment, as if she'd forgotten there were only three of them now. "Go and fetch her. Bring some food, too. I'll harness the dogs."

Mila felt cheered despite the reason for their journey. Though she loved the forest, she hadn't been looking forward to sleighing for a whole day alone. As she trudged back to the house, she scanned the encircling tracks, and beyond them, the larch trees. Bare and pale as bones, they swayed in the icy wind, and seemed to stare back.

CHAPTER FIVE

Traps

*M*ila's cheeks sang with cold, a cold that reached long fingers down inside her throat and up her nose with every breath. Dusha and Danya were doing well, pulling them fast through the snow, driven by a worrisome energy Mila felt under her own skin: a dark fizzing, like a hot coal spitting. She and Sanna kept up the rhythm, pushing with their feet off the snow to help the dogs along, both of them bobbing down, then swooping up.

The sleigh was running as well as the dogs. Made of light, unpainted birch, Oskar had renewed the iron on the bottom of the runners only the month before. He'd cut himself, he'd made them so sharp. There were two driving bars, one at the front and one at the back, with planks to stand on. Pípa sat in the wide sealskin bed, braid flying, while Sanna and Mila stood at the back for better balance, keeping the reins loose and long.

They passed the first four traps without slowing: three hare snares beneath a light dusting of snow and leaves, the bait frozen, and one deadfall set at the right height for foxes, who were too clever to step on disturbed ground. Oskar was catching less and less, and Mila thought of what the man had said: *Perhaps it is only that the forest has given enough.* She trembled.

Their father had laid the traps as straight as the trees would allow, in a direct path to his favorite place, and Mila imagined Oskar scuffling to check them, further and further into the forest. But he was not here now, nor was there any sign he had been since the night's snowfall.

She chewed the inside of her cheek. What little of Sanna's face she could see was taut, her lips a dark line. Mila wanted to slide her hand along the bar, to grab her sister's, but she didn't want to risk losing her grip. Besides, she was still annoyed at Sanna for thinking Oskar would leave willingly, and for saying she would leave too if she had the chance.

A twist of bitterness spiked her stomach as Mila ducked low beneath a grasping branch, feeling it catch momentarily on her cap before whistling past her ear. They passed half a dozen more snares and two hidden pit traps before the forest started its true gathering together, the trees closer, the pale sky more and more a far-off thought, puzzled to pieces through closing branches.

She could still remember a distant spring, before Pípa was born, even before her own name-gifting, when they had walked this same path. Her father had hoisted her onto his back, low-hanging leaves brushing her head. They'd passed through a wall of close trunks, and there in front of them was a mighty birch: the heart-tree. It grew unnaturally broad, more akin to an oak, as wide as their house and as high, it seemed to Mila, as the sky. Its leaves formed a blanket over their heads, moss carpeting their steps. Wildflowers grew in the patches of sun, bright splotches of red and purple that threw up a honeyed scent.

Papa had set her gently down. *Race you.*

They'd climbed, all of them breathless and laughing, higher and higher, Oskar and Sanna recklessly fast. Mila's heart pounded but she wasn't afraid, not with Mama close behind. It was a perfect climbing tree, the whorls of the bark soft but strong, fitting her small hands exactly.

When they reached the top, all Mila could see was forest, her whole world a tangle of wood and leaves. She had never felt so happy.

This is the most special place in all the forest, Mama had said. *It's the tree about which all others grow. See how the other trees swirl around it, like a snail shell, protecting it?* Mila turned carefully, following the spiral until the shape was lost. *In return, it protects us, makes sure the forest provides for our way of life.*

Eldbjørn lives here, Oskar had said, reaching across to pinch Mila's arm. *Here comes the mighty Eldbjørn—*

Planting human hearts like corn, Sanna finished. *Let's hope he's not hungry,* she'd teased, pinching Mila's other arm.

Leave your little sister alone, said Papa with a sigh.

Mila had looked at him. *But we take sap—doesn't that make him angry?*

We don't take more than we need, said Mama.

But Mila was not reassured. *Eldbjørn doesn't really kill anyone who hurts the heart-tree—he's just a story, isn't he?*

He'd only hurt people to protect the forest, said Mama. *Either way, the heart-tree is precious. If it were harmed, the forest would die.*

And we'd have to leave, said Papa sadly, and Mila leaned against his side. She had learned her love for the forest from him and Mama both.

But that won't happen, will it?

Of course not, said Mama gently.

And you'll never leave?

Mila had heard the smile in Papa's voice. *Never.*

He had, though, and winter had stayed as long as he was gone, like he'd taken the sun with him. Mila hadn't climbed a tree since.

They were nearing the last of the traps, nearing the grove of birches that surrounded the heart-tree. Mila could see them—thin silver spirits in the low winter light, shining against the dark bark of fir and larch. They seemed smaller than she'd remembered, and duller, though she supposed she was simply bigger. The coals beneath her skin hissed again. *Never harm the heart-tree. Eldbjørn will get you.* Their father had repeated this so often it had hooked into their minds long before they'd been name-gifted.

Sanna saw they were close too, and clucked her tongue at the back of her throat, pulling on the reins to slow Dusha and Danya. They obeyed instantly and slowed to a gentle walk, their breath flying up in great clouds.

Mila jumped from the sleigh to walk beside them, her hand on Dusha's high flank. She was warm even through Mila's glove, and Mila could feel the buzz of her breath, like a hive in the hollow trunk of a tree. Sanna stayed on the sleigh, shifting to the center to balance it.

"*Stuta!*" Sanna lingered on the *s* sound between slightly parted teeth, like the whistle of their battered kettle, and the dogs stopped.

Mila did not. She passed beneath the final trap, a series of noose snares covered in a night's frost, laid at steady intervals along the frozen branches, hopeful of birds. Papa had told them how once the whole forest was filled with wings. Though she remembered some of their life before, her memories were patchy and she could not recall such an abundance. *Their song used to wake me!* he'd say. *Can you imagine?*

Mila could never imagine.

One trap was laid low and Mila lifted it, finding the smear and body of a young shrike, barely bigger than a fledgling.

"Mila?" Sanna's voice was gentle.

"See how small it is?" murmured Mila over the muted rustle of the forest, the soft pant of the dogs. "Only good for baiting."

She crouched, legs sore from the sleigh, and prodded lightly at the bird. The feathers gave a little beneath her fingers. The bird was not frozen, which meant Oskar had not missed it from a previous visit. But it also meant he had not come to the traps today. He was not here.

"It's fresh?" asked Sanna.

Mila nodded, sharp tears gritting the corners of her eyes. She wiped them away impatiently and strode onward, the final few strides that took her into the grove, to where the heart-tree grew. A tree that was taller and older than any other in the forest, stretching out its mighty branches until it seemed the whole sky was heart-tree. . . .

But what Mila saw brought her to her knees.

CHAPTER SIX

The Heart-Tree

*B*ehind her, Sanna gasped and even Pípa, who had never been here before, cried out.

"What's happened?"

The heart-tree, once the tallest in the forest, ended at head height, bark peeling off in great reams. The trunk lay at an angle, like a giant brought into a crashing slumber. It had been hacked across the roots, the wounds stark and pulpy, its white insides shining, long-frozen sap dried and gleaming like honey mixed with freshly spilled blood. Ice had wormed inside and shattered the slices wider. Around it, the other birches seemed to be leaning toward it, like mourners bowed by a burial pit.

There was no telling how long it had lain like this. Winter caught everything in slow time, even death.

The heart-tree had been felled.

Mila's mind was racing. *Who has done this?* The sight sent fear and grief deep inside her bones. *Why?* Mama's story came again and again to her, how Eldbjørn lived here, and how his living as the tree kept the forest alive.

The stranger's cruel smile flashed into her head as a light hand rested on her fur-swathed back. Had *he* . . . ?

"Milenka—" started Sanna, but Mila flinched away as though her sister had struck her.

"Don't call me that," she hissed, feeling the fear in her belly grow claws. "I told you he'd been taken, and now we've wasted all this time, nearly a quarter-sun, when we should be going after them."

Sanna's face drew in, shadows pinching under her high cheekbones. Her voice was still gentle when she spoke. "I knew it was stupid to come, stupid to give you false hope—"

"You're the stupid one!" shouted Mila, making Danya whine and Pípa flinch. She kicked at a drift, sending powder flecking up into her sister's thin face. "Oskar hasn't gone, he's been taken!"

Sanna reached into her pouch and pulled out something glinting. "The ring—"

Mila knocked her hand, sending the ring spinning into the snow. "It means nothing!" she yelled. "Oskar wouldn't leave!"

Pípa stooped hesitantly and picked up the ring from where it glimmered, like a drop of blood, in the white. "Why do you have Oskar's ring?"

Neither sister answered her, eyes fixed on each other's faces. Pípa was too young to remember that it had been Papa's before Oskar wore it. She slipped it onto her thumb.

"Careful, Pípa," Mila said spitefully. "You might leave too."

Pípa frowned as the shadows in Sanna's face grew darker still. Their eldest sister narrowed her ice-blue eyes before turning away to the sleigh. "We have to go. It tastes like snow."

Mila felt it too, the clean cold under her tongue, the snap of the air around her exposed ear lobes, but she flushed hot with fury. She bent and picked up a handful of snow, throwing it hard at Sanna's back. It struck her squarely on the nape of her neck beneath her still-perfect bun, and slid down inside her cloak.

Sanna wheeled around, striding back to her, cloak swishing. She stopped so close Mila felt her breath, her fists clenched. Mila saw her own anger matched in her sister's face. "You think now is the time for a snow fight? You're acting like a baby, like Pípa—"

"Hey—" Pípa protested.

"And *you* are acting like Papa!" screamed Mila.

Sanna's jaw clenched. "What's that meant to mean?"

Mila swallowed the lump in her throat, willed the tears back down. "You've given up. You've given up on Oskar, just as Papa gave up on us."

"Milenka." Sanna reached out again, and Mila flinched. "Oskar's the one that's like Papa, not me."

Mila stepped back, shaking her head. "You didn't see him by the window. Someone was talking to him. Someone was scaring him."

"It's true," said Pípa. "I saw him too."

The forest was quiet for a second, Sanna looking at both girls. Her expression was inscrutable, but when she spoke, her voice was soft. "Perhaps it was you who scared him, little mouse. You know how good you are at sneaking." A faint smile tiptoed at the corners of Sanna's lips, but her eyes were sad. She held out her arms to Mila. "You probably startled him while he was making plans to go."

Mila let Sanna hold her. She felt suddenly very tired, limbs drooping like snow-weighted branches. She took a deep breath. Sanna smelled of the wood fire at home and the sharp tang of birch-tar soap. The same as Oskar had when he'd hugged her last night. Mila cleared her throat, pushing gently away from her sister, and forced herself to look her in the eyes.

"I want to go to Stavgar." She kept her voice deliberately calm. Shouting hadn't helped sway her sister— she had to try a different tack.

Sanna's dark eyebrows knitted. "Why?"

"It's not far if we cut through from here," said Mila, pointing at the thinner trees to their right. "The men said they were heading north, so they must've passed through Stavgar if they were taking the fastest route. If we . . ." Her voice trailed off as Sanna gave a loud tut.

"Mila, we are not going after him. If he didn't want to stay, then good riddance."

"If they passed through Stavgar, we'll know whether Oskar was with them or not."

As if she could hear the silent accusation, Sanna threw her hands up. "Look, Mila. It's going to snow soon. If we go to Stavgar, we'll barely make it home before full dark."

"But we will if we go now."

"I can't risk being out in the dark with Pípa—"

"I don't mind," said Pípa eagerly. "I like the dark." Of all of them, she was in some ways the bravest.

"See," urged Mila. "Don't you want to be sure?"

"I'm already sure." Sanna sighed. Mila stayed quiet. She could tell Sanna was thinking it over, or she'd have already turned the dogs for home. Finally, her sister nodded.

"Fine," she said, on a great exasperated exhale.

Mila did not stop to savor the victory, only hurried to the sleigh. Sanna led the dogs in a small semicircle to face north, and she barely gave her sister time to secure her hold on the sleigh handle before snapping the reins.

"*Farash!*"

CHAPTER SEVEN

The Cord

The track to Stavgar was covered in deeper snow than the path to the heart-tree, though the thick forest canopy had saved them from the worst of it. Before the endless winter, it had been the main trading route, along which precious goods like wool, copper, or iron-work came from the north, or salt, fish, and fine cloth from the south. Now it was mainly used by the Orekson siblings, venturing to Stavgar for meat when the traps failed, or by Geir, visiting Sanna under the pretense of delivering knives.

Occasionally, when the snow eased a little, traders still passed by, so if Sanna needed a new pot when the old ones were finally blackened beyond belief or thread when gut would not do for mending, Oskar had to be roused at the crack of dawn to stand at the crossroads, swaddled in furs, and wait. Despite the early start, Pípa and Mila would accompany him as often as they were allowed. Mila liked to see the outer boundaries of her forest and wonder at the southern people, who sometimes had hair the color of sunshine, even paler than Geir's, or the tall men who kept their beards plaited and beaded in a style she heard used to be all the rage in the north.

More precious than silk thread, or salt, was the gossip from the mountain city by the sea, where Mama had grown up. Bovnik had almost as many mines as Eldbjørn had trees, and it overlooked the Boreal Sea, where now the magical island of Thule was said to be caught in the ice, trapped by their eternal winter. The town of Bovnik was built so high up, Mama had said that, in the days before winter, the mountains pierced the sun at sunset and sent its light dripping down the pale buildings like egg yolk. Once Bovnik had been a thriving place, but they'd heard that since winter began the mines had become treacherous, and now the town was all but abandoned.

It was at the trading crossroads that Mila saw something in the snow. A faint glint, like grit in a wound.

"*Stuta!*"

She was not prepared for the sudden halt. The handle jabbed into her ribs as the dogs obeyed her even though Sanna had the reins, and Mila felt a stab of satisfaction at their loyalty.

Pípa tumbled sideways, and Sanna pitched forward, nearly tipping over the handle. "*Javoyt!*" she shouted, rubbing her stomach. "Are you trying to kill us?"

Mila kept the smile from her face. "I . . . I wanted . . ." But she'd lost the spot where she'd seen the glimmer. The snow shone a uniform grayish-white as she scanned it.

Sanna's face softened. "The snow will have covered their tracks, Mila."

Mila nodded. "I'll just have a look."

Sanna let out another sigh. "Quickly, before I change my mind and turn us home."

"As if the dogs would listen to you over me," muttered Mila under her breath.

"What?"

"I'll be quick."

Mila jumped off the sleigh and cast her eyes over the snow. It lay across the path like a sheet, ruching gently where tree roots lay.

"What're you looking for?" asked Pípa. Mila only shrugged. Perhaps she had imagined it. Nothing seemed out of the ordinary, but as Mila turned back toward the sleigh, she noticed a root had worked its way to the center of the path. She scuffed her boot over it, and it rolled under her foot. It was not a root at all.

Sanna was stamping her feet and tutting. "Come *on,* Mila. Or I'm taking us home. Three . . . Sit down, Pípa!"

Mila ignored her. She bent down and brushed the snow aside. There! The glint against the white. She looked around quickly. Sanna was pointing to the seal-skin bed on the sleigh, where Pípa waited, her other hand on the reins.

"Two . . ."

Gold cord. It was a piece of the gold cord the stranger had worn around his boots—the same cord all his men had worn. Mila hesitated. She didn't really want to touch it, even with gloves.

"One! That's it, we're going home."

"No, I'm coming." Mila picked up the cord and put it in her cloak before she could think better of it. Her heart thrummed.

This time it was Mila who was caught unawares when Sanna shouted, *"Farash!"* Her sister's sly grin as she scrambled to grab hold made her glad she hadn't shown Sanna what she'd found. She would dismiss the gold cord as nothing, but Mila could feel it was important.

Sanna thought she knew best, thought she knew their brother, thought he thought like she did. Mila looked ahead at the running dogs, and beyond, into the winter-caught forest. Soon they would be in Stavgar, and Sanna would know the truth—that Oskar was nothing like her or Papa, and everything like Mila.

—————

Snowflakes dappled Mila's face just as Stavgar began to reveal itself, signs of civilization coming slow as a thaw through the trees. It had been a year at least since Mila had visited, and little seemed to have changed. Several livestock pens dotted the route, with low-slung turf out-houses.

Sanna slowed the dogs to a walk, and jumped down to stretch her legs. Mila did the same, to spare the dogs. The path was cleared of snow, but they had run for hours now without a rest. Mila ran her hand along Danya's back, feeling the slick nubs of spine.

"They're tired," she said. "And we're almost there. Let's stop for a bit."

"Did you bring food?" asked Sanna, and Mila remembered the dried elk strips she'd packed into her cloak. She pulled out a handful and passed some to Pípa and Sanna before holding one in each palm and letting the dogs chomp them down. She tasted one herself, the tough saltiness comforting, as she glanced around the low banks edging the road. A prickle of fear crept up the back of her neck.

"Sanna?"

"Mm?" She had her mouth full.

"Look where we are."

Sanna looked. Mila watched her stop chewing, her cold-flushed cheeks paling. Immediately she took up the reins and nodded for Mila to get on the bed beside Pípa. "*Farash,*" she muttered.

"What is it?" Pípa asked, peering around, and Mila felt her little sister's sharp inhale of breath. Crouched in a turn of the path was a building so overgrown it seemed more forest than house. It slunk low to the ground, like a beast stalking prey, turf roof sagging in the center, bowed by bare vines that muscled up like thorns.

"Is that . . . the mage's house?" Pípa whispered as Sanna ordered the dogs on.

Mila nodded. The mage of Stavgar was as much fable as flesh: a boy with magic, never grown, hardly ever seen. She had never seen him herself, only heard stories from Geir, but those were enough to make her cross her fingers against dark magic. Pípa's cloak pocket bulged, and she knew her sister had done the same. They rounded a bend and the house slid out of sight.

"Do you think he saw us? Can he put the evil eye on us?"

"Hush, Pípa." Mila put her arm around her little sister. "It's only stories."

Just a different way of telling the truth. Her mother's words conjured themselves, and Mila pushed them away, sent them spinning from her in a puff of cold breath. She didn't want to dwell on such an icy truth.

CHAPTER EIGHT

Stavgar

More dwellings began to line the road, and at last they reached the square, where the jarl—the ruler of the town—and other wealthy villagers lived in houses with richly carved lintels and stone-slab roofs. One whole side of the square was taken up with the meethouse, a huge structure with wooden pillars striping its side.

"They sound like they're celebrating," said Sanna, and Mila heard raised voices coming from within. Now that they were here, her dread for Oskar returned in full force. What if no one had seen the man and boys pass by? Or worse, what if they had, and Sanna was proved right?

The square was swept clear of snow and gravel gritted the icy ground, making it easier to walk but harder to sleigh. The sisters clambered off, Mila's legs stiff and complaining as blood rushed back into them, and Sanna tied up the dogs at a long trough opposite the meethouse.

Dusha attempted to lick the frozen water, snuffling plaintively as her tongue rasped on the ice.

"Stop, you silly goose," said Mila, cracking it with her elbow so the dogs could drink the water beneath the icy pane. She placed her hand on Dusha's ruff, the ground swaying around her. Soon they would know the truth of it. Sanna seemed so sure. *So I must be sure too.*

Mila squared her shoulders and followed her sisters to the meethouse door: a massive, whorled slab of oak with an iron ring for a handle. Sanna had stopped short, and Mila saw that she was pinching her already-flushed cheeks and checking that her brooch was straight.

"Really, Sanna?" Mila's lip curled in disgust. "You're worried about Geir seeing you?"

She pushed past her sister without waiting for an answer, feeling the cold of the metal even through her fur-lined glove as she heaved the door open.

The enormous fire at the center of the room was blazing, flames leaping higher than the heads of the people crowding around it. A wall of heat hit Mila's frozen face, bringing the blood tingling to her cheeks, and she pulled off her hat as her scalp began to itch with sweat.

It was only when she looked up from stowing it in her pocket that she realized the room had fallen silent, and that every face was turned toward her. The man nearest her called, "It's just the Orekson girls!" and the room broke into noise again.

Mila pulled on his arm. "Excuse me, I was wondering if—"

But at that moment, the meeting bell was struck. A low, sonorous ripple spread around the walls, followed by silence. Mila looked at the speaking platform, a raised jut of wood reached by steps struck into the loam wall.

A woman in a green cloak stood there, her hand on the bell's tongue. Mila recognized her broad, handsome face. Bretta, the town's jarl.

"Enough bickering," said Bretta, in a voice as low as the bell's. "I will listen to petitions one at a time, but to save tedious details, here are the facts I think we all share. At dawn, fourteen boys rode into our square—"

"Fourteen," hissed Mila to Sanna, who had moved to stand beside her, Pípa at her other side. "There were thirteen that came to our home. Oskar must be with them."

"Shhh!" snapped Sanna. "I'm listening."

"They wished to trade for supplies for their journey north. As is customary, we invited them in here, and sent for the men to welcome them to our town."

"And boys," wailed a pitiful voice. Mila craned her neck and saw a copper-haired woman, face twisted and tearstained. "My boy Geir has gone."

"Oh, Sanna!" Pípa raised her hand to her mouth, and Mila looked quickly at her sister. Sanna swayed, grasping Geir's brooch. Mila took Sanna's other hand and squeezed it tightly.

"Your son is seventeen and so nearly a man," snapped Bretta. "He is responsible for his own foolish choices. I myself met with their leader." She gave a nearly imperceptible shudder. "And he told us of their journey. The riches they had seen, and were to return to . . . He claimed to have more treasure at his home, greater than any other."

Her voice sounded wistful. "It sounded like fantasy to me, especially coming from such a ragged bunch, and I thought the boys would see through them just as I did. I was wrong." She drew a shaky breath. "The town's boys are gone, all of them."

"Was my brother among them?"

Sanna's voice made Mila start and pull her sweating hand away.

"Who spoke?" said Bretta sharply, and the crowd parted like cracking ice.

Sanna stepped forward to stand beside the fire. It lit her black hair a shimmering blue. Mila felt rooted to the spot.

"I have come from the south forest. I'm Yelfer Orekson's eldest daughter."

"Ah, yes," said Bretta. Her tone was instantly disapproving. Their father's abandonment was well known here in Stavgar. "And your question?"

"Was my brother with them? Oskar." Sanna's voice shook. Mila felt a rush of sympathy and pride—her sister was still strong, despite the news of Geir's desertion.

Bretta regarded her keenly. "I could not say. His companions were hooded. Is your brother gone too?"

"Yes."

"Selfish boy," said Bretta bitterly. "Aren't you only sisters without him?"

Sanna nodded. "So they—the boys—they weren't taken? They weren't forced to go?"

Bretta shook her head, and Mila felt as though she stood on a precipice. Her head wheeled. It could not be true.

"They went chasing treasure," Bretta said with contempt. "It seems it is always a man's lot to leave, a woman's duty to be left."

The men in the room shifted uncomfortably under Bretta's sharp gaze.

"I wouldn't be so certain that they went willingly if I were you." A new voice, light and almost singsong, came from a dark corner beside the oak door.

The room seemed to move as one animal, shrinking back, as a short, cloaked shape stepped forward into the firelight's reach. The man beside Mila spat, and she saw his wife cross her fingers. A chill, fine as a cobweb, seemed to fall across them all, and a boy stepped into the light.

CHAPTER NINE

The Mage

He was barely taller than Mila, and not much older. His fine white-blond hair settled like a cloud about his shoulders, his tatty robes of dark blue a little long. Mila could not help but recoil when he looked up. His eyes were pale as moonstones.

"Is he blind?" she heard Pípa whisper to Sanna.

Though she had spoken so quietly that Mila had barely heard, his eyes flicked to Pípa, and he shook his head. A web-like chill cracked into scuttling spiders of fear across Mila's neck.

"You were asked not to come," said Bretta. Even the indomitable jarl seemed nervous of him. "We told you to stay away."

"I have something to say, if you would hear it." The voice was whisper-light but commanding. "I said it would happen. I said it was only a matter of time until he came."

Bretta held a hand up. "Please, Rune. We don't need a story now."

Rune . . .

This skinny boy was the much-feared mage of Stavgar? Though his agelessness was well known, she'd always imagined him as imposing as an oak. Here he was, looking like not more than a couple of years separated them. They were even a similar height.

Rune smiled, showing gappy teeth. "Who said anything about a story? He came, you saw him. You spoke with him."

"I speak with many people," said Bretta, her tone making it clear her patience would not hold much longer. "If you have something to say, say it, simply and fast."

"They did not go willingly." Rune had turned to Sanna, who flinched. "The Bear took them."

The pennant fluttered in Mila's mind—a bear beneath a tree rooted in gold. She slipped her hand inside her pocket, gripped the cord. It felt strangely warm.

"I saw no bear," said Bretta. "What bear?"

"He keeps himself hidden," said Rune, still staring at Sanna. Mila drew closer to her sisters, and Rune's eyes moved to her. "It takes a special kind of person to see."

"Enough!" Bretta snapped, and Mila jumped. "I saw no bear, I saw no struggle. I saw only boy after boy chasing adventure at the cost of family."

Mila suddenly did not want to hear it—any of it. All she wanted was the quiet of their home, the forest surrounding, Oskar cracking wise and her sisters making her laugh. Oh, for last night's argument! What she wouldn't give for boiled cabbage now. She wanted to be with the dogs, at home, with Pípa and Oskar and—

She gave a great sob. "Sanna," she gasped, and fell to the reed-strewn floor, her legs and chest aching. Sanna and Pípa knelt down beside her, and the jarl joined them.

Mila blinked, trying to clear her hazy head. The jarl was even more impressive up close, her nose straight as an arrow, her thick brown eyebrows like fletches, her eyes gray flint.

Bretta considered them a moment. "You can't stay in the forest alone. You can stay in my home. Go there now." She raised her hand and her voice so the whole room could all hear her: "We will weather this together."

"Thank you," said Sanna, bowing her head.

Bretta turned back to the hall, and Sanna began to help Mila to her feet. Mila felt herself about to fall again, but a bony hand, surprisingly strong, supported her under her armpit.

"You saw," said the singsong voice.

"What are you doing?" said Sanna harshly, pulling Mila away from the mage.

Mila met the milky eyes, and it seemed as though Rune spoke directly inside her head. "You'll find me in the first house."

It was only Sanna's reply that made Mila feel sure Rune had spoken aloud at all: "She'll not be coming to your house, nor speaking to you. Leave us alone."

It had stopped snowing, and Dusha and Danya were chomping on the icicles that hung from the side of the trough, lips pulled back from their teeth. Normally their daftness would make Mila smile, but now she felt a hollowness like she never had before. Not after Mama. Not even after Papa.

"That's the jarl's house, isn't it?" Pípa was pointing at the second-largest building in the square: a sturdy, stone-walled house with a door painted bloodred. They knocked and a servant opened it, standing aside once Sanna explained why they were there.

Mila let Sanna guide her into the jarl's house. She felt thick furs under her booted feet, and the warmth of the fire as Sanna placed her gently before it. Pípa crept to Mila's side and began fiddling with Papa's ring, which was still on her thumb. It made Mila sick to look at it.

"You think we should stay?" Pípa asked.

Sanna sighed. "It seems sensible."

"What if Oskar comes back? He won't know where we are."

Sanna clenched her eyes shut in a way that told Mila she did not think he would ever come back. Her hand toyed with Geir's brooch, still pinned to her cloak.

"If Oskar returns from the north, he will pass through Stavgar anyway," she said at last. "We can decide what to do then. It's only a quarter-sun sleigh home after all."

There fell an unsteady silence, and Mila realized Sanna was going to say nothing of the boy with the moonstone eyes.

"What about the mage?" she asked.

"Yes, was that him?" Pípa said, digging a sharp elbow into Mila's side to hoist herself more upright. "Are mages the same as witches?"

"Witches aren't real," snapped Sanna. "And mages aren't really real either. They're mad, people who believe themselves magic. They have some knowledge of herbs, and I heard Rune's mother was respected by some in her day." Her wrinkled nose showed she was not among them. "But Geir said"—Sanna looked at her lap, and Mila saw the glint of tears in her eyes—"Geir said he's practically a lunatic. So whatever Rune told you, forget it."

"He's only a boy," said Mila, shuddering. "I thought—"

"Unnatural beast," hissed Sanna, but Mila could sense fear under her sister's disgust. "Why didn't he go too?"

They fell silent. Oskar and Geir's absence seemed to swell to fill the gap. At long last, Sanna stretched wearily, and yawned.

"Bed now, I think."

They all climbed into their furs, and Mila's heavy body dragged her down, down, sleep covering her as fully as snow over tracks.

CHAPTER TEN

The First House

*F*ind me in the first house.

Mila's dreams had been full of the mage's words, and she woke knowing what she must do. Sanna and Pípa were still sleeping when she sneaked out. First she went to the dogs, to check that they were settled into the kennels. It would have been quicker to sleigh, but Dusha and Danya would be excitable, leaping up to lick her face and barking. Mila knew they'd make a racket if she harnessed them outside.

She looked over her shoulder. No one was following, and no faces looked out from the ice windows of the turf houses. She lengthened her stride. Only yesterday they had hurried away from the mage's house, crossed their fingers against it. And now here she was, hurrying toward it.

Besides, her legs had lost their aching and were filled with a restless, twitching energy. She hoped the walk might tire them. Her stomach felt filled with moths, darting around a bright point of hope that Rune might be able to tell her something about Oskar.

On either side, the trees leaned in and whispered. She wished they could speak, wished they could tell her what they'd seen the night Oskar left. *Was taken*, she corrected herself, though Bretta had seemed certain they had gone willingly, and the jarl was the sort of person whose opinion felt like fact.

Mila thrust her hands into her cloak pockets, and instantly pulled her right hand back out. It felt as though she had grasped an icicle. She'd forgotten about the cord. Bile rose in her throat when she saw it was no longer gold and pliable, but as twisted and dark as a thick, dried root. It sat rigid in her hand, emanating that vicious cold, as if it were a living thing that had been plucked, and was now shriveled and dead.

Mila shivered, but she did not throw it away. Instinct had led her to find it, and instinct told her to keep it. She put it back in her pocket, and continued walking, keeping her right hand warm in her left armpit. She didn't want to touch the cord again.

Finally, the bank to her left rose, and the turf roof of the mage's house peeked over the top. It still felt to Mila that the house was poised, ready to move, like in the story Papa had told her about the witch whose house had hen's legs. As Mila drew closer she heard singing, misty as a chill morning. She scrambled up the bank, her boots skidding on black ice, and listened.

At home you sleep,
At home you're safe,
Until a face
At the window calls.

Heart pounding, she moved to the iceless window, the cold nipping her ears as she lifted her hat to hear better.

It knows your fears
And if it knows your name,
You can't turn your face
From the winter's call.

The singing stopped. A moment later, the unpainted door opened. "Winter-well-met, Mila."

Sanna might believe witches only existed in stories, but Mila felt as though she were in a fairy tale now, one that would not end well for the child about to enter a stranger's house, even if the stranger seemed to be a child, too. For some reason, the mage's young appearance only made his old age all the more uncanny. Mila saw now that his eyes were not completely white from pupil to lid. It only seemed that way because his irises were the palest gray-blue, like river ice. He was perhaps only half a hand taller than she, and his white-blond hair was neatly combed now, less a cloud and more a smooth slice of moon.

Mila took a deep breath and stepped inside.

"Welcome," said Rune. "Shoes off."

Mila unlaced her boots and placed them by the door, accepting the soft felt slippers Rune held out.

There was just one room, and the house felt even smaller than it looked from the outside because it was so full of things. Glass vials—real glass!—of all sizes were scattered haphazardly over every surface, the dark wood table, bench, and fur-strewn bed. Bunches of herbs swayed from beams that shuddered when Rune closed the door behind Mila.

A fire hissed and spat in the back corner of the room, and above it, set into the wall, was another grate that filtered the flames and left only smoke rising to the chimney. The smoke was the palest white, like wisps of mist, and smelled of apples.

Above the smoke hung several slabs of fish. From their pink flesh and size Mila guessed they were salmon, even though only the richest could afford such things. She had tried it just once, a petal-thin, rose-colored wafer that Mama had served one spring equinox, accompanied by heart-tree sap sweet and golden as honey.

"Don't mind the mess," said Rune, expertly picking his way to a chair beside the fire. "I'm not used to visitors. Come. Sit."

Mila followed his path to the fire, trying to stop her cloak from catching on the objects she had no name for.

"Ouch!" She stepped on something small and hard, and lifted her foot to see two bone dice inscribed with symbols.

"Sorry," said Rune, with a sudden bark of laughter that made his face open and kind. He held out his hand for them. "I was scrying." He threw the dice straight in the fire.

"Oh!" said Mila. "Did I break them?"

"No, no. I just need to renew them. You'll have confused the runes—they aren't used to feet."

Mila stared at him. "Do you . . . live here alone?" She looked around at the clutter. "No grown-ups?"

"I'm quite grown-up enough, thank you," said Rune, not unkindly. "Besides, would a grown-up let you do this?"

He reached into the fire with his bare hand, and even as Mila cried out for him to be careful, he fished out two smoking dice and placed them on the fur hearthrug. They began to smolder and Rune batted them with his sleeve a couple of times.

"I am so glad you came, and so soon," he said distractedly. "Because there is very little time, and I am only allowed to ask you thrice."

Mila blinked away from the dice and the singed fur, and focused again on the strange boy. "Ask me thrice?"

"To come. Otherwise it means you do not want to be here. And if you do not want to be here, it means you are not willing. And if you are not willing—"

"Willing?" said Mila, looking around nervously. What if Rune wanted her to participate in scrying, or some other dark art that Sanna definitely wouldn't approve of? Not that she would approve of anything Mila was currently doing, or seeing.

"If you are not willing," continued Rune gently, "you do not have the heart for it."

"Heart for what?"

"For what I am about to tell you," said Rune slowly, as though Mila were Pípa's age. He reached for a glass bottle of amber liquid and unstoppered it. Mila smelled something strong and sweet. "Do you want some mead? I find it invigorates the heart."

"I'm only twelve," said Mila.

"It's not strong." Rune shrugged and swigged.

Mila raised one eyebrow the way Sanna had taught her.

Rune made a *pfft* sound, blowing air from his lips. "Milk, then? I have some fresh from my goat."

Mila felt she was the wrong age for milk, too, but she nodded, and Rune maneuvered his way to the opposite corner, beside the back door. With a flourish, he removed a woolen blanket from a large black goat. Mila raised a hand to her mouth, startled, and Rune held a copper pan under the goat's udder.

"Come on, Lunka, be nice."

The goat bleated once, then went back to chewing the straw laid before her. Once the pan was filled, Rune threw the wool back over the goat and returned to the fire, suspending the pan from two hooks over the flames.

"Be ready in a minute," said the boy, as though having a goat covered with a blanket in your house was the most ordinary thing in the world.

Mila gaped, wondering again if she had made the right decision to come.

"Now," said Rune, taking another swig of mead. "We may as well get started. As I said, there's not much time left."

"Time left before what?"

"Before you lose your brother forever."

CHAPTER ELEVEN

A Between Place

Mila felt a thump in her chest, as if her heart were reminding her to breathe. "What do you mean? Do you know where he is?"

"You saw, you see. You knew your brother hadn't gone of his own accord, that—"

"He had been taken." Mila finished the sentence with him.

Rune nodded. "Just like all the others. Taken by the Bear."

"Do you mean the stranger?" said Mila. "Is that his name?"

"It's the name others gave him," said Rune. "You'll have heard his story, no doubt, but perhaps you know that story by another name: Eldbjørn, the guar—"

"The guardian of the forest." Mila gasped. She felt as though Mama were reaching through time and whispering her story in her ear.

Rune nodded approvingly. "What do you know about him?"

"That he is a bear, and he lives in the . . ." She hesitated, the horrible vision of the birch grove ghosting into her mind. "In the heart-tree, and protects the forest."

"Protects the forest, yes, that's one way of putting it," said Rune thoughtfully. "At all costs."

Mila flinched, "What does that mean?"

"That he'll destroy anything that harms the forest," said Rune. "And people do tend to harm things, don't we?"

Here comes the mighty Eldbjørn, planting human hearts like corn, chorused Mila's mind unhelpfully, before she could stop it.

Rune sang again.

It knows your fears
And if it knows your name,
You can't turn your face
From the winter's call.

"If it—he—knows your name . . ." Mila faltered.

"He can call you," said Rune. "Control you. People give their names away too easy. They don't understand there's sense in the old traditions, in naming your children falsely until the evil eye passes over. Do you have your true name yet?"

Mila nodded.

"Shame. It's easier if you don't know it. Then it's harder for him to find it. You must keep it hidden from him, or else there would be no point in helping you follow those boys."

Mila was about to tell him that if they were right, and that man had been Eldbjørn, then he already knew her name: that Oskar had told him her name back on that first meeting. But the mage was saying Mila couldn't go if the Bear knew her name, and she couldn't bring herself to stay put any longer. So she swallowed the sentence down. He didn't need to know everything, and anyway, he was hardly answering all her questions in a straightforward manner. "Follow where?"

"North."

"Yes," said Mila impatiently. Rune's roundabout way of talking might suit stories or songs, but it was very annoying. "But where north? Where has he taken my brother? And the others?"

"To Thule, of course."

Mila sat back in her chair. She could believe that a threatening stranger had managed to kidnap her brother; she could believe, having seen the size of him, that he was called the Bear. But Eldbjørn? The spirit her Mama had told stories of? And now she was being told that he lived on Thule—the magical island trapped by winter? That was surely nonsense.

"I can see what you're thinking." Rune's gaze was suddenly focused and sharp. "That Thule is a fairy tale. But if you go back far enough, fairies lived to tell their own tales. Some of us understand that impossible places are possible."

"But Thule isn't a real place," said Mila, exasperated.

Rune placed his thin hands one over the other. "There are many realms, Mila, seen and unseen. They overlap a bit like fish scales. Sometimes they intertwine." He laced his fingers.

"But no one's ever been there."

"That's where you're wrong. Plenty go . . ." Rune's gaze went far away, as though he stood on a hilltop. "But very few return."

Mila frowned, remembering what Sanna had said. "Why weren't you taken with the other boys?"

"I'm not a *boy*, Mila." He spat the word like it was something beneath him, and Mila reminded herself that she was talking to someone older than the trees. "I'm a mage. I have ways to protect myself."

"And why not the others?" Mila's anger flared hot as flame.

Rune sat back suddenly in his chair, as though Mila had pushed him. "I tried to warn them!" His voice was full of hurt, almost sulky. "But you saw how they talk to me. Bretta has never liked me. They treat me like a diseased animal, or else like a mad child. There's no respect here for the old ways."

"But why?" cried Mila. "Why does he take them?"

Rune relented and leaned forward, firelight spreading over his thin lips, narrow nose, huge moonstone eyes. He seemed to Mila at once as young as Pípa and as ancient as time.

"Because he wants you gone from the forest, Mila. He wants you humans *dead*. That's why he brought the winter, and sent spring to Thule for himself, that's why he takes the boys—"

"*He* brought the winter?" Mila gasped. Rune sat back and nodded gravely. "Why?"

"Now, that is a true mystery," said Rune. "I have my theories, though."

"Tell me," said Mila.

"They need more thinking. But one thing is clear." Rune stared into the fire. "We have to find a way past winter."

"What is that supposed to mean?" Mila had had enough. She threw up her hands and made to stand, but Rune held out a pacifying palm.

"I know you're feeling like what I say does not make sense, Mila, but doesn't it make more sense than what your sister believes happened—that your brother left you?"

Mila felt a thin thread in her chest break, the thread that had held together her trust in Sanna.

"Yes," she said, simply.

The boy smiled. "I knew you saw. You care, Mila, deeply, and that makes you pay attention. There are things in the world that you have to look at with more than your eyes, hear with more than your ears, touch with more than your fingers. *You* can do that. It's what makes you similar to the Bear, in a way—"

"I'm nothing like him!"

"You're fierce," continued Rune. "You'll do anything to protect what you love, I can see that in you. And that makes you dangerous to him. By coming here, by realizing the Bear was more and worse than a man—that shows you can bring your brother back."

Hope must have shown in Mila's face because Rune continued solemnly, "But you do know, if you want him back, it won't be easy? It will be the opposite of easy. It is a dangerous journey to Thule. And you don't have much time."

The air no longer smelled of apples, but of burned milk.

"How do you know all this?" Mila said, her voice barely above a whisper.

Rune turned his face full to the fire. "I'm a mage, Mila. I can read patterns, sense truths." Watching his silhouette, Mila realized she believed in him. She wasn't sure quite why she did, with his frosty eyes and slippery words and a goat in his house. But she felt that he was good. Still, Rune was holding something back some other, deeper honesty he was not ready to share—she could feel that, too.

He turned his strange eyes upon her. "I know most fear me, even despise me for my ways. But this is just what I am. We must leave for Thule tonight, if you want your brother back. And we cannot tell anyone where we are going. They will only try to stop us."

"We? You're coming too?" Mila felt something a little like relief, though she was not sure Sanna would approve of her going on the journey with the mage. Then again, Sanna would not approve of her going at all.

"I always intended to."

Mila hesitated. Did she really believe what Rune had told her? An immortal named the Bear, causing an everlasting winter, coming to take boys. A magical island. Wasn't it simpler to believe that Oskar had tired of their life and gone seeking riches?

Simpler, and harder.

She felt she should ask for some sort of proof of all the impossible things the mage had told her. But hadn't she felt something was different—dangerous, *difficult*—the moment she'd seen the stranger? His silencing of the dogs, his feet atop the snow, bound in gold, his sudden sinking down.

Stories are just another way of telling the truth. And here she was—at the heart of the story, where it mingled with truth. She decided to believe.

"I found something," she said, pulling the cord from her cloak. "But it wasn't like this when I got it. It was . . ."

She trailed off, because Rune was looking at the cord with triumph flashing across his face.

"I told you," he said in a hoarse voice. "I said you could see."

Mila held it out, but Rune drew back, shaking his head. "No, no. You must keep it. Bring this, and something of your brother's, something he wore and loved."

"I have his hunting knife." She pulled it from her belt to show him.

"Good," said Rune. "Do you suppose your family can spare a dog and sleigh?"

"Dusha will be able to manage us both," said Mila. "If we don't bring much."

"We don't need much. Leave me in charge of food and supplies," he added, suddenly practical, "and meet me at the top crossroads at high moon."

He rose, and Mila did too, her blood pounding as she crossed the cluttered room to pull on her boots.

"And, Mila?"

She paused in the doorway, the cold biting her cheeks.

"Don't let anyone see you leave. There can be no delays."

Mila nodded, and the door was closed behind her. She scuttered over the bank and back to the road. Her breath was as loud as a westerly wind in her ears.

I'm going, she thought, to make it real. *I'm going to save Oskar.*

CHAPTER TWELVE

Lies

*I*t had taken Mila's best lying face to convince Sanna she had not been at the mage's house.

"Where were you, then? You weren't with the dogs, I checked."

"I was"—Mila thought quickly—"climbing."

Sanna narrowed her eyes suspiciously. "Climbing? You haven't done that since . . ."

Papa left passed silently between them. It was true: Now it was Pípa who was the best climber, the one who could walk branches like a path. Mila nodded, her insides wrenching with guilt as Sanna's face softened. She knew her sister was mourning not just Oskar but Geir as well.

I'm lying for them, she reminded herself. *So I can bring Oskar home.*

They passed the day quietly, Sanna compulsively sweeping their spotless room, Pípa and Mila playing games beside the fire. Mila was just beginning to lose hope that she would have a chance to make an inconspicuous exit when there came a knock on the door.

"Winter-well-met," said Bretta, striding in without waiting for them to answer. Mila supposed it was her house she had loaned them a room in, but she could not help but feel a spike of dislike for the jarl. Bretta seemed so pleased with herself. "I've come to ask you to join us in the meethouse for dinner."

Sanna half-bowed and said, "Thank you, Jarl Bretta."

Pípa caught Mila's gaze and rolled her eyes.

"Wonderful," said Bretta grandly, and looked them all over. "There are fresh clothes in the chest."

She strode out again, leaving the door wide open. Mila got up and closed it as Sanna started fussing over her reflection in the ice window.

"I look a mess! Mila, fetch me something, would you?"

Mila heaved open the oak lid of the chest and found fine woolen dresses of green and gray. She pulled out a green one with yellow stitching and passed it to Sanna.

"Aren't you two changing?" said Sanna, fussing with her hair.

"I need to wash," said Mila, indicating the jug and basin in the corner. "Why don't you go ahead? I don't want you to miss any of the feast."

"Pípa needs a wash too," said Sanna decidedly. "You two hurry up, though."

Sanna looked almost happy as she threw on her cloak and left the room. *She always seems happier around other people,* Mila thought, with a twinge of hurt.

Pípa slid off her perch by the fire and went to tug on Mila's hand. "She doesn't seem too sad about being here, does she?"

"She's just looking forward to a feast," said Mila, something in her chest softening as she crouched beside her youngest sister. "She's hungry. I am too. I'm mostly sad, though."

"Me too," said Pípa, her wide brown eyes looking around the chamber. "I want to be at home. And I want Oskar to be there."

"Píp?" In that moment Mila longed to tell Pípa. But she knew her sister would cry, and insist she didn't go, and tell Sanna, and then they'd never get Oskar back. "I don't feel like washing any more. We can just say we did."

"Good," said Pípa, who hated being clean.

"Do you want me to plait your hair?"

"Yes," said Pípa, throwing herself down on the bearskin. "But not so tight as Sanna does it."

"Don't you enjoy your scalp being lifted off your skull?" teased Mila, and Pípa twisted around and crumpled her little face in a look of disgust. "I'll be gentle."

She combed her fingers through Pípa's hair. It was threaded with auburn, like her own and Mama's, but with Sanna's soft straightness—Mila had always envied her sisters for that. Mila felt a plunging in her stomach. Her going would be hardest of all on her little sister. Pípa was quiet on the rare occasions they came into contact with other children, and she had a tendency to stare, which even Mila found unsettling sometimes. And Sanna had less and less time for her.

She cleared her throat and said, "Do you like it here, Píp?"

Pípa's thin shoulders shrugged. "I'd rather be home. I wish things were like normal."

"With us arguing over a cabbage?"

Pípa giggled. "With us, and Sanna not so mean, and Oskar . . ." Her high voice went higher still. "Here. Or there. Oskar home. Mila . . . it's not my fault, is it?"

Mila stopped untangling. "What do you mean?"

"Well, Papa going was my fault, wasn't it?"

Mila reached her arms around her little sister and pulled her onto her lap so she could look down into her worried face. Pípa's lip was wobbling.

"Why do you say that?"

"Because Mama died having me." Pípa's eyes were bright. "And Papa left because Mama—"

"It's not your fault. Mama was sick before she had you," said Mila fiercely, squeezing Pípa so tight she squirmed. "None of this is your fault." She pushed her gently upright, keeping her tone brisk even as she blinked away tears.

"Promise?"

"Promise." She sectioned Pípa's hair into three and smoothed it over her shoulders and back. It fell to the floor, pooling in Mila's lap. A few slow moments passed. "What do you think happened, Píp? To Oskar."

Pípa held her breath in the way she always did when she was thinking hard. She held it so long Mila wondered how she didn't faint or go red. Finally, the breath came gushing out as she said, "I don't think Sanna and Bretta are right."

"You don't think he would go?"

"No," said Pípa in such a decisive voice it made Mila's heart swell. "I don't think he would leave us. Maybe he'd leave Sanna, because she's so grumpy. But you and me and the dogs? He loves us."

Papa loved us too. It didn't stop him.

"How much longer?" said Pípa impatiently. "My neck is aching."

"It's because you slouch," said Mila, taking up the sections of hair and beginning to braid.

Pípa sat up straighter, and Mila could see the ring glinting on her thumb as she toyed with it. They sat quietly a moment, Mila looping strand over strand.

"You think so too, don't you?"

"Think what?" said Mila.

"That he didn't want to go."

"No," said Mila, trying to sound as certain as her little sister. "I don't think he did."

"What are we going to do about it?"

Mila's fingers turned all thumbs, and the center section slipped. "If there was something to be done, would you do it? If you were older, I mean."

"Of course. And why would I have to be older?" said Pípa, her voice frowny. "The grown-ups aren't doing anything."

Mila's heart was beating very fast. Of course she couldn't tell Pípa. Whatever she thought, she *was* too young to go with them on what was sure to be a dangerous journey. And Rune had told her not to say anything to anyone. She finished braiding and held her hand out over Pípa's shoulder. Pípa handed her two bone pins and Mila slid them crosswise to hold the plait in place.

Pípa spun around on her knees, the braid whipping around so Mila had to lean back. "Careful!"

"You're not going too?" Pípa's dark eyes were wide. She leaned forward so Mila could feel her hot breath, her small hands pressing hard on Mila's shoulders. "You'd tell me?"

"Yes," Mila lied, trying not to blink or fidget or do any of the things that would give away the truth. Pípa looked deep into Mila's eyes with a face so serious she looked far older than her seven years of winter. Mila almost laughed. Finally, Pípa sat back.

"All right." She jumped to her feet. "Shall we go and find Sanna? I'm hungry."

"You know what, Píp? I think I do need that wash after all," said Mila, fetching her sister's cloak from its hook.

"But you said—"

"I know," said Mila briskly, fastening it under Pípa's chin. "But I feel all grimy. You go to the meethouse. I'll follow."

Pípa sighed like Sanna. "All right."

She left without a backward glance, and Mila held her arms stiffly by her sides to keep from running after her and hugging her tight.

"Goodbye, Píp," she whispered.

CHAPTER THIRTEEN

High Moon

The lie souring in her stomach, Mila took one last look around the room, then hurried out into the night.

The path to the dog shed took her past the square, and she hugged the shadows. She could hear voices coming from the meethouse, and as she stood shivering, waiting for a moment when she could cross the square unseen, she imagined her family inside, warm and fed.

Mila felt such a pull of love it made her belly ache— though that may have been partly hunger. She should have gone for an early dinner. It suddenly all felt impossible and silly.

Since Papa left, Mila had spent her days thinking things through. Overthinking, really. She no longer delighted in climbing trees, like Pípa, or plunging into icy rivers, like Sanna. She was content to watch, listening to stories of other people's adventures.

Because adventurers were nothing like her. They were not afraid of heights or cold, fast-flowing water. Sanna would be a far better rescuer. Even Pípa had stronger nerves. But Mila was the one going. And perhaps that was enough: to be the one who believed. What had Rune said? The one who *saw*. She had seen what no one else had—she had seen the Bear first, had seen him seem to hover on the snow, weightless despite his bulk, had seen Oskar talking to him through the ice window.

And while she thought about it, wasn't she being brave right now? She remembered Mama's words. *The softest, and so the strongest.* She ducked her head and ran full pelt across the square, hoping no one was watching from the high, small windows. She reached the kennel and pulled the door open.

There were perhaps twelve dogs in the cramped space, and when she slipped in they surged toward her, leaping and whining. Dusha pushed forward and made high-pitched sounds, leaping to lick her face.

"All right, Dusha," she murmured. "Hush now, hush."

The other dogs quieted when they realized she had not brought food. Mila ran a comforting hand over Danya, who looked unimpressed by the other dogs' lack of restraint. She lowered her face to his ruff and hugged him close. "Be good."

"What are you doing?"

The voice was quiet, but Mila jumped as though it had shouted. She had not heard the door open, and she turned quickly. Pípa was there, her fierce face pale and all angles in the moonlight, her arms heaped with bread. Mila's heart sank.

"Píp, I'm—"

"Are you going somewhere?" Pípa eyed the harness in her hands, which Mila tried to hide behind her.

"No, I'm not—"

"You said you wouldn't go!" Pípa's voice rose tremulously, and Mila hurried to shush her. "If Sanna hadn't sent me with food for the dogs, you would have gone without me! You lied!"

"I couldn't tell you," said Mila desperately. "Please, Pípa, don't tell anyone."

"I won't," said Pípa determinedly. "Because I'm going with you."

"No."

"Yes," said Pípa. "Or I'll scream."

She took a deep breath and held it. Mila felt as if she were about to scream herself. "You can't come with me. It's going to be dangerous—"

"You're going after Oskar." It was not a question, but Mila nodded anyway. "He's my brother too. And you're my sister. You have to take me with you."

Pípa dropped the bread and the dogs surged forward again to chomp on the black loaves. Pípa pulled the harness from Mila's hands, but Mila held tight.

"I can't take you, Píp. You're too young—"

"I'm tall for my age," snapped Pípa.

Mila tried to think as she wrestled the harness free of Pípa's grip and led Dusha outside to where their sleigh sat beside several others. She pulled back the sealskin covering and Pípa immediately sat on it.

"The load's too big for Dusha," snapped Mila. "And you're making me late."

"Late for who?"

Mila said nothing.

"You're not going without me," said Pípa fiercely. "If you do, I'll tell Sanna straightaway and we'll come catch you."

"Then we'll lose Oskar forever!"

"I'm coming." Pípa's lip wobbled. "I'll follow behind with Danya if you kick me off the sleigh. I'm coming."

The moon was fully up. Mila looked at her sister's determined face in the moonlight, and could not think what to do. She could lock her in the dog shed, but Pípa would scream and set the dogs barking, and that would quickly bring the others running.

"Please," she said to her sister. "It's too dangerous for you to come."

Pípa stared at her, her face implacable. "I thought you were going to be late." She pulled another bread roll from her cloak pocket and took a noisy bite.

Letting out a hiss of frustration, Mila harnessed Dusha to the sleigh. She thought a moment, then went back into the kennel to fetch Danya and harnessed him alongside his sister. With one more venomous glance at Pípa, she pushed off into the night. Things were already not going to plan, and she hadn't even left yet.

The meethouse was still bright and loud, and she steered them in a slow circle, keeping it out of sight. Pípa was silent as snow, and they reached the northern path. At the crossroads, Mila's heart sank. There was no light, no movement. But suddenly a crouched black rock shifted, and Rune's face looked up at them. He grimaced.

"Who—?"

"My little sister," said Mila apologetically.

"Little? She's taller than you." Mila glared and Rune sighed heavily. "This isn't a journey for little ones."

"You just said I'm tall," said Pípa, her eyes flashing.

The two stared each other down for a moment, then Rune suddenly reached out for Pípa's hand. "Is that yours?"

"My brother's," said Pípa, holding up her hand for him to see the ring better. "And my Papa's."

"Shiny," said Rune, looking thoughtful.

"You can't have it."

"I don't want it." He turned to Mila. "At least you brought two dogs." He slung his bundle onto the back of the sleigh and it clinked.

"I'm Pípa."

"Rune. Is that bread?"

He settled beside Pípa, and Mila took this to mean the first driving shift was hers.

"Well," said Rune, taking the roll Pípa held out to him. "Northward we go."

Mila took a deep breath and watched her exhalation smoke in the high moonlight. "*Farash!*"

The dogs gave a great leap forward and began to run.

PART 2

North

CHAPTER FOURTEEN

Shadows

*F*rost glittered like finery on the bare branches of the trees; the night air was crystalline and bright. The stars were as thick as clouds above the branches, bunching over Mila's head.

She felt a bony hand on her shoulder, and out of the corner of her eye saw it was Rune, steadying himself.

"You're an excellent sleigh-driver."

"The road is good," Mila replied, the cold scratching her throat. Here the banks rose high on either side, and the snow had fallen and compacted between them, the sleigh's runners cutting it easy as a warm knife through butter.

"How far to Thule?" She felt ridiculous asking it, speaking the name of a story-island as though it were a real place. She might as well ask him how far to the moon. But they were going somewhere, and she had to believe there was something at the end of their quest.

"We must head for Bovnik first," said the boy mage. "It is our only path to the island."

Mila's heart leapt at the mention of her mother's city. She glanced at Pípa's huddled form. Perhaps she could leave her little sister there—it would likely be safer than bringing her on the rest of the journey. "All right, then, how far to Bovnik?"

Rune moved to stand at the rail beside her. He took one of the reins to balance the sleigh better.

"Three days' solid ride."

Mila frowned, or at least she thought she did. Her forehead was numb. "The dogs will need to rest."

"I will help them," said Rune. "They will not need sleep."

"Will it—won't that hurt them?"

"I thought we had decided to trust each other?"

Mila was not so sure about that. But she supposed something in her must trust him, or she would not be here, on this sleigh, riding to the top of the world, where the Bear waited. A thin keening came from the east, as if the wind were crying. A wolf.

She looked across at Rune. His moon eyes glittered. "We will make it in time."

"How can you be so sure?" said Mila impatiently.

Rune's thin face hardened.

"All you need to know—and trust—is that I want to help you, and that I can. I would not have given you hope if I could not get you there in time. But getting you there is all I can do—after that it's up to you."

"What will I have to do?"

"You'll know."

Mila highly doubted that, but in place of a reply, an enormous yawn heaved itself out of her chest and stretched her mouth wide.

"Go and rest," said Rune, slipping the other rein from Mila's grip. "I will wake you at sunrise."

Mila's eyes felt incredibly heavy all of a sudden. She made her careful way to the back of the sleigh, where Pípa lay piled beneath furs, her head on Rune's pack. Mila eased herself alongside her, and watched the forest whip past, trees as dark and high as walls.

Rune was whispering to the dogs, and the sleigh gave another wrench forward. Mila jammed her feet against the guardrail. They seemed to be going even faster now, star streaks raking against the black-blue sky, but Mila was too weary to ask how Rune had managed it.

The trees were ghostly blurs. Mila turned her head to try and catch one in stillness, flicking her eyes back and forth, but it only made her dizzy, her eyelashes casting shadows at the corners of her vision. Then the shadows shifted, and a vast dark shape was moving between the trees, almost as fast as the sleigh.

Mila sat up as though hooked on a fishing line, a bitter taste filling her mouth. She stared at the trees again, searching for the shadowy shape. It was gone. Her heart thudded against her ribs. She had seen something, hadn't she? A wolf, perhaps . . . like the one she'd heard . . . but no. It had been too large, had moved with a lolloping stride.

A bear?

Pípa stirred in her sleep and Mila put a hand on her sister's warm side, feeling the soft rise and fall of her breath. Mila tried to slow her gasps to match as she stared out at the pale forest. She'd imagined it. She must have. She lay back.

The night was the same color as Sanna's hair, and Mila felt a stab of guilty satisfaction. It was Sanna who had always wanted to get away, and now she was the one left behind. Mila turned onto her side and curled against Pípa. Her little sister's hair had come loose from its plait and tickled Mila's nose. Finally, Mila closed her eyes and let the to and fro of the sleigh rock her to sleep.

—⟫⟫—

She woke in early morning, the darkness lifting to let the sky lighten to gray. As her body stretched its way out of sleep, Mila realized that they were not moving. *It must have been stopping that woke me*, she thought. She lay looking at the sideways trees creaking on either side of a wide track, then lifted her head to turn them upright again.

It all felt too still.

"Rune?" The boy mage was standing hunched at the reins, and the dogs were whining their warning growl.

"Stay down." Rune's tone was muted, as though he were trying to speak without moving his lips.

"What is it?" said Mila, instantly afraid, remembering the shadowy, lolloping shape. She peered past Rune and saw a figure standing on the path before them.

The figure was tall, thin, cloaked, and unmoving as a tree. A person? It was so still it was hard to believe it was living. But somehow she knew it was.

The path was wide enough for two sleighs, but the figure stood in the very center. They could not pass unless it moved.

Before she could take a closer look, Rune pushed Mila back down with his boot. "Shh," he said harshly, out of the side of his mouth. She could feel his fear, and fell backward into the furs, massaging her shoulder, but did not cry out.

"Can I help you, friend?" Rune's voice was as sharp and clear as frost.

No answer came. Rune hesitated a moment, then urged the dogs on at a walking pace. "I need to pass this way. Would you mind stepping aside?"

Mila noticed Rune had said "I." He was trying to make the person believe he was traveling alone, with only the dogs for company. She felt Pípa tug on her arm, and slid under the fur with her, holding her finger to her lips.

The last time she and Pípa had lain silent like this was when they had seen their brother at the ice window.

Mila raised the furs a little, looked under the rail. She could see only the figure's legs. The bottom of the cloak was covered in ice, so thick she could make out the crystals bonded on top of one another, even at this distance. How long had the person been standing there? A small breeze flapped the long dark cloak about the figure's ankles, and Mila's eyes caught a flash of gold. He was tied with golden cord.

CHAPTER FIFTEEN

The Bound Boy

*H*er heart seemed to freeze. The figure was too small to be the stranger—the Bear, she reminded herself—but there was cord around his legs. . . .

No. Mila looked more carefully as the cloak stirred in the wind. Only one leg was bound. As she saw this, Mila felt something hot pressing into her side. Trying to move as little as possible, she reached inside her cloak and gave a small hiss of pain. The cord in her pocket was hot to the touch, like an ember pulled from a fire.

She took it out quickly, protecting her fingers with her cloak, and even by the gray light filtering through a narrow gap in the furs, it was obvious the cord was once again shining and golden as heart-tree sap. What had made it change? This person?

"What's that?" whispered Pípa, but Mila only clamped her hand over her sister's mouth.

"Please, move aside so I can pass," came Rune's voice again, but this time there was an undertow to his tone. Mila felt her own fear rising with Rune's. She pushed the golden cord back into her cloak and reached for Oskar's knife at her belt.

They were three sleigh-lengths away from the figure before it finally spoke, in a deep, deliberate voice that sent icicles lancing into Mila's chest.

"I'd not go any further."

It was the Bear's voice, she was sure of it. But this figure was not him—she could make out a smooth chin, a child's face on the verge of manhood. He seemed to be a boy not much older than Oskar. How did he have the Bear's voice? Mila strained to hear over her sister's rabbit-scared breaths.

"*Stuta,*" murmured Rune, bringing the dogs to a halt several paces away. "I must, friend. My route is north."

"Why are you traveling north in such cold? It's not safe for young ones."

"I am not so young," said Rune. Mila could tell he was trying to sound jovial, but his voice shook.

"Those two can't have seen many more winters between them than I have."

"They're old enough in dog years," tried Rune, as if he was referring to Danya and Dusha, though the pretense was clearly useless. This person knew Pípa and Mila were there. The gold cord seemed to grow even hotter, its ember heat flaring. Mila kept her grip tight on Oskar's knife.

"Still," said the boy in that terrible voice, "one of them's old enough to be a thief."

"We've nothing of yours," said Rune. "Let us pass in peace."

"Only if Mila gives me back what's mine."

Three things happened then, all at once.

Mila clasped a hand to her temple as she felt a stab of pain. Rune threw something—what, Mila had no idea; all she saw was the mage's hand arcing up. There was a smashing sound, and something black and glittering was falling about the boy's ankles, starting to sizzle in the cold air. She smelled a chemical sharpness.

Smoke engulfed the figure, which began to cough and double over, and Rune yelled, "*Farash!*" and Dusha and Danya began to run so fast and so suddenly it was as though a mighty current had them in its grip.

She and Pípa were thrown flat onto the sleigh's bottom, and Mila kept her hand pressed to her head, eyes wide. It was similar to the pain she'd felt when Oskar had given her name to the Bear, like ice-head, the sort of pain she got from melting snow in her mouth.

The bound boy was not moving out of the way.

Worse than that, he was *trying* to move. He coughed and tugged at his unbound leg, but now that they were nearly on top of him, Mila saw it was not only his cloak that was icy—his legs were too.

He was frozen in place.

Rune seemed to notice at the same time. The mage tugged hard on the dogs' left rein, trying to steer around the figure, but the dogs swerved so sharply that they sent the sleigh skidding sideways toward him. Pípa screamed.

Mila closed her eyes as she felt rather than heard two sickening thuds as the sleigh's iron-clad runners hit the person, one after the other. The sleigh jerked up, and down, but did not break. Her own body rose briefly into the air, clear off the sleigh. When she fell back hard, she was numb to it.

All she could think of was binding Oskar's hand with lichen salve and balm leaves the month before, after he had cut himself sharpening the metal strips to make the sleigh grip better and run smoother. The runners were sharp as blades, and the sleigh was heavy with them and their supplies.

Rune swore and pulled the dogs to a stop. Pípa stopped screaming. Mila listened to the silence yawning beyond the caged drum of her heart. The cord in her pocket was cold again.

The boy had not even cried out.

—>>>—

After what felt like hours but was only the length of one of Pípa's held breaths, someone gently lifted the furs off Mila.

"Don't look," said Rune, and his voice was as sad and tired as his crumpled face. "I need my spare cloak."

Mila could not think of anything worse than looking. She hated blood. Even binding Oskar's wound had turned her stomach, yet she'd done it anyway. Somehow still, as in a night terror, she felt compelled to look the horror full in the face.

She pushed herself up, her back sore from the jolt of the collision, but Rune blocked her view with the cloak.

"No," he said, more firmly. "There are some things, Mila, that once you see them you cannot unsee, however much you wish it. You do not have to look."

"It's our fault," Mila replied.

"It's *my* fault," said Rune, and through her dull shock Mila saw that there were tears running down the mage's cheeks. "But his face . . . he looked relieved. The Bear had him. That's why we heard the Bear speaking, and now this boy is at peace. You had nothing to do with it."

"I did," said Mila. She pulled the cord out of her pocket. "He wanted this. Perhaps if I had given it to him—" Her throat tightened around her words.

"Hush," said Rune, and he put his arms around her and squeezed. He smelled of green spice and smoked apples, and she felt comforted. "He was left here for one purpose only. To stop us."

For that to happen, Mila thought, *the Bear must know we're following him.* A splinter of fear lodged in her spine as she pressed her face into Rune's cloak. She could not bring herself to ask the mage to tell her whether she was right.

"He tried to move," said Pípa. She was staring past them, and with horror Mila realized she was looking at the bound boy's body. "He was trying to get away."

Rune pulled Pípa to him as well, spreading his arms around them both so the whole world was full of just the three of them, facing each other in the silent forest.

"This shows you what we are dealing with," said Rune. "The cord controls them, just like the names. Which reminds me"—Rune's voice became harsh—"you lied to me."

Mila blinked up at him, at those strange eyes, nearly light as snow. "I—"

"You did not tell me he knew your name."

Mila remembered the pain in her head, just before they struck the boy, triggered by her name in his mouth. Hot shame warmed her cheeks.

"I didn't lie, exactly."

"But you didn't tell the truth," said Rune gravely.

"You said you wouldn't help me!"

"And I wouldn't have."

Queasiness planted its rocking foot in Mila's stomach. "You . . . you aren't going to take us back?"

Rune looked at her for a long moment, then let out a longer breath. "No. But, Mila—there can be no more lies."

"I'm sorry."

Rune nodded, and squeezed her shoulder lightly. "You two stay here. I'll be done in a minute. I'll move him off the road, cover him with snow. It's the best we can do."

Pípa lay down in the sleigh. She was pale and trembling, and Mila again felt an awful guilt at allowing her to come. She took her sister's hand and curled up next to her, tried not to listen to the dogs whining, the sound of something heavy moving across the ice. Tried not to smell on the clean, fresh air the warm, metallic scent of blood, underlaid by the tang of whatever Rune had thrown at the figure. She clutched the cold cord and her sister's cold hand and tried to think of nothing but *cold, cold, cold* until Rune tapped her lightly on the shoulder. "It's done."

Mila looked instinctively at the mage's hands, but they were bare and washed with snow, no stain or mark on them. He held the gold cord from the boy's leg, which Mila knew would soon start to stiffen into its dead-root state.

"I thought it might be useful," said Rune. "I think you should keep it with the other."

"Can't you—" started Mila, and immediately heard and hated the whine in her voice. "All right." She hurriedly slipped the cord into her cloak.

Behind them, Rune had swept fresh snow over the path. Only a shadow remained, sitting under the white like a slow-rising bruise. The sisters hugged each other close, Rune clucked his tongue, and Mila watched the patch of risen snow, set back from the road and topped with a cairn. Just before it disappeared out of sight, she thought the shadow stretching from under it moved. She shook her head, squeezing her eyes so tight stars danced inside her eyelids.

CHAPTER SIXTEEN
The Chase

They rode silently for another hour or so, until Pípa's stomach gave such a mighty rumble Rune heard it from the front of the sleigh.

"*Stuta.*"

The mage rifled through his bags, and produced three parcels. He gave one to each of them, and Mila unwrapped it to find a crispbread and a whitish-yellow slab of a bitter-smelling cheese, which she assumed was made from Lunka's milk.

Rune sprinkled a little blackish-red herb on top of his own crispbread, but on the sisters' he put something purple.

"What's that?"

"Moonroot."

"What's it do?" asked Pípa.

"It's soothing," said Rune. "It'll help with the shock. I use it after a bad dream. You can also stuff a handful in your ears, and it blocks out all manner of sounds. It even stops me from hearing Lunka snoring."

"Who's Lunka?" asked Pípa.

"His goat," said Mila impatiently.

"Goat?" giggled Pípa. "You have a goat in your house?"

"You don't?" said Rune, waggling his eyebrows. Pípa shook her head, delighted. "How strange."

Mila waved her hand to get the mage's attention back. "Why do you have a different herb?"

"It's flameberry, for energy."

Pípa bit and chewed. "It's good, Mila! Like salt, almost."

Mila could not think of anything she'd like to do less than eat, but Rune noticed her hesitation and looked at her sternly. "You must be strong, Mila. You must eat."

She bit into the cheese and crispbread. Pípa was right: It was beautifully salty. Rune nodded approvingly and bent to give the dogs some dried strips of meat, which he also scattered with flameberry.

"Is that—" Mila started, though Dusha was already wolfing hers down.

"It's safe," said Rune reassuringly. He laid a careful hand on her shoulder, his young face grave. "We're on the same side, Mila."

She nodded, cheeks flushing as she felt his pale eyes on her. His hand steadied her, her trust in him almost as firm as his grip. He made her feel safe, even though he appeared to be scarcely more than a boy. Maybe *because* of it.

"Shall I take over the reins?" she asked, brushing crumbs from her cloak when they were finished.

"No," said Rune. "The flameberry will help me."

Dusha was in a playful mood, snapping at Danya's heels and mock-growling. The flameberry had obviously helped them, too. She wanted to drive the sleigh again, to feel in control, but she looked at Pípa, who was still pale. Her little sister needed her more than the dogs did. "Sit with me, Pípa?"

Mila slid back beside her little sister. Within moments of the dogs starting to run again, Pípa was asleep, her breath warming Mila's cheek. The trees whipped past overhead, making the light flicker, and when Mila closed her eyes she could almost imagine they were home again, with Oskar and Sanna, all lying together in front of the dancing fire.

———≫———

There was heat on her cheeks—the sensation so forgotten and unfamiliar Mila did not immediately know it as different from cold. She placed her hand on her face and opened her eyes, but everything was so bright and searing she closed them instantly.

Something was wrong.

Mila blinked carefully. She could feel that they were moving, but she couldn't tell from looking—no trees passing, no branches whistling past. The world was bright, as though they were moving through the heart of a snowstorm, but there was warmth on her face. The world was not white at all—it was burning.

Her forest was on fire!

Mila pushed herself up with a yelp, and saw then that she was mistaken. The forest was not on fire, because the forest was not there at all. She steadied herself against the sleigh, willing herself to see the world as it was, things as they appeared.

There *were* trees, but they were sparse and scattered. Behind them, the thick line of the forest was far away, like a retreating tide. A vast stretch of white sloped before her, dotted here and there with boulders and scraggy trees. Ahead was a peak, black as a fin and high as the heart-tree. It was dizzying, almost sickening. For the first time in Mila's life, she could see for miles without a tree blocking her view.

And there *was* fire, but it burned from the torches tied along the sides of the sleigh, and Mila now saw why they were lit. Amongst the scarce trees, black shapes darted, drawing closer and closer to the sleigh. A howl went up.

"Wolves!"

Mila hadn't meant to shout, but fear had gripped her throat and forced the word out. She tasted the metal of her fear as Rune turned.

"Oh, good, you're awake." He sounded strangely calm. He still stood at the front rail of the sleigh, stiff as a statue. In front of him, the dogs cut a deep path through the snow, dark bodies reassuringly solid against the white.

Mila felt winded, though all she had done was sit upright. The world had altered so entirely in the few hours she had slept. The forest was gone, the winter sun pale in the paler sky. Pípa was still sleeping.

"Wolves!" she repeated, pointing.

"What do you think the torches are for?" said Rune. She could tell he was trying to appear calm but sensed his concern was rising.

Mila stumbled to her feet. The world tipped again, the incline steep and unforgiving on the swift sleigh. Mila's legs went from under her, and she fell back again.

"What's wrong with you?"

"What's wrong with *me*?" Mila spat the horrid taste in her mouth over the side of the sleigh, ducking between the torches. "What's wrong with *you*? Why didn't you wake us? How long have I slept for?"

"A bit over a day," said Rune. "You must have been tired." He flicked a look over his shoulder. "They're getting a bit too close for comfort."

She followed Rune's gaze. The wolves were no longer scattered amongst the far-off trees, but were running in a fast-closing semicircle, maybe a hundred feet behind.

Dusha and Danya were practically flying—Mila had never seen them run so fast, especially not sleigh-laden and uphill, but still they were no match for—*five, six, seven, eight!*—hungry wolves. The wind blew up behind them, and she could smell the tang of them, even over the torches—the sweat-and-stale-blood excitement of the hunt. Mila looked more closely at them and her breath caught in her throat.

"Their eyes! They're—"

"Gold," said Rune, almost to himself. His face went even paler. "*Javoyt!* They're his!"

"What do you mean?" Mila said wildly, though she already knew. She could feel the cords glowing again at her side.

"He's possessed them, like that bound boy!"

Mila looked from the wolves to Pípa, still deep in a moonroot sleep. She'd promised Mama she would protect her sister, and she must. She glanced ahead, to her dogs bounding through the snow, then scanned the peak. It was steep and impenetrable. She squinted against the cold wind stinging her eyes, and there! A small gap at the top. A thin imprint sunk between two crests, like the gap between Pípa's front teeth, supporting a ceiling of snow. She felt a surge of strength move through her.

Mila rushed to the front of the sleigh. "Move!"

Rune looked sideways at her, frowning. "What?"

"Give me the reins," she shouted, and yanked them from his grasp. He gripped the rail to keep from falling as she pulled the dogs hard to the left.

"What are you doing?"

She ignored his question and called back, "Grab a torch!"

"Mila—"

"Just do it, Rune!"

When Mila blinked, the path she was aiming for disappeared as if it had never been—but with the next blink it was back, a mere speck in the distance. Mila adjusted the reins, pulling the dogs slightly more to the left. "*Farash,* Dush-Dush! *Farash,* Danya!"

Dusha gave two great barks at the sound of her voice, and the dogs' ears went back. They sped as fast and straight as spears, the points of their noses arrowing forward. Mila chanced a look around, and immediately wished she hadn't.

The wolves were barely twenty paces behind, and as the incline became steeper, they seemed to speed up, leaping chaotically over one another, gold eyes flashing. Rune was crouched by Pípa's head, untying one of the lashed torches from its rope.

Mila could see her sister was now awake and gripping tightly to the sleigh. "Stay down, Pípa!"

"Come on, come on." Rune was fumbling with the torch. One of the wolves drew level with him just as he slipped it free. "Aha!"

"Get him!" yelled Mila, and Rune thrust the flame at the wolf. It spun away, yelping, and there was a brief smell of burning fur.

She pulled her gaze back to the path, correcting Dusha and Danya's direction. They were getting close to the path, and Mila could see more clearly the great slab of snow overhanging it, creating a tunnel for them to pass through and down the other side of the mountain.

Mila ground her teeth. A snarl came curling into her ear and she looked to her right. A lone wolf galloped alongside, gray and black, yellow teeth bared. Mila had a soft spot for wolves. Though they rarely sighted them in Eldbjørn forest, they looked so like her beloved dogs, only thinner and fiercer. *But these are the Bear's*, she reminded herself.

She steered the dogs quickly right and then left, sending the sleigh whipping sideways. She felt a small *bump* and her stomach soured, remembering the two awful thuds—but the wolf yelped and fell away. When

Mila looked back over her shoulder she saw it stop completely, but it was still standing, still alive.

"Well done," cried Rune. "But they're gaining!"

In front, the path was seconds away. Behind, the wolves were just as close. Mila clenched her jaw so tight she felt her teeth lock together. *This had better work.*

"Ready?" she called.

"For what?" chorused Rune and Pípa, fear apparent in both their voices. Mila nodded, determined, though she did not know what for. A moment later they were beneath the powdery snow of the overhang.

As they passed beneath it Mila shouted again, *"Farash!"* and the dogs pelted on.

The ground dropped away beneath them and Mila felt the weightlessness of flight as the sleigh's momentum sailed them downward. She held tight to the handle of the sleigh with one hand, and with the other raked her arm through the overhanging snow. It hit her arm like rock, but then it loosened, and gave, blocking the way through behind them.

There was a burst of white light, so bright Mila could taste it. She heard Pípa scream and she forced her eyes open, looking for her sister. Before she could spot her, the ground rushed up to meet them.

CHAPTER SEVENTEEN

Buried

*S*now in her nose and mouth, snow in her ears and eyes. She was drowning in it. Mila spat and worked her hand free from where it was clamped to her side, bringing it up to clear a hollow beside her mouth so she could breathe. She scraped snow from between her lips and gums, and snorted to clear her nose. All around her was dark gray, the color of light gulleted through thick snow. *Where is Pípa?*

Her heart was pounding, and the blood rushed to her head. Something was pressing around her neck, and she realized her cap had slipped backward, the leather tie tightening around her throat. *Breathe*, she thought, but it was just as irritating and unhelpful as someone else saying it.

Remember what to do. Oskar's voice floated to her on a tide of panic. *If you're buried in a snow crush, the first thing to do is find out which way is up.*

She forced herself to think clearly. *Which way is up?*

Mila cleared a bigger hollow by her mouth, and spat again, this time paying attention to where the spit fell. It dripped sideways, toward her left cheek, which meant that that was downward. She flexed her trapped legs, and they responded. Her ribs ached, but her limbs seemed unbroken. Her thick layer of furs must have helped.

Make space for yourself, gently, so the snow doesn't pack tighter. Move your arms and legs as if you're making a snow bird. She remembered Oskar demonstrating, laughing as she kicked snow over him to rebury his limbs.

She began to gently work her own limbs back and forth, freeing them. Her breath was coming faster and faster, but she forced it into a steady rhythm. Being buried in snow was like being trapped in earth and drowning in water—she had air, but it was limited. She had movement, but it was limited.

Move slowly, and keep your breathing calm.

Once her legs were loose enough, she drew them up to her torso, wiggling her toes to get the blood moving.

At least she still had both her boots—if she made it out of here, she would need her feet, and in snow a lost boot meant a lost foot.

I need to get to Pípa. A gasp gripped her throat, a burst of missing so sharp it seemed to pierce her skin. She forced it down and began to wriggle away from the direction her spit had fallen. Upward.

Using her hands like shovels, she swept the snow sideways so it dropped downward. There, she kicked it into compact ridges and used her feet to push off them, until she was climbing the hollow left by her body.

It felt achingly slow, but Mila counted to one hundred, and counted to one hundred again, and at two hundred and forty-three her hand was gripped by biting cold, and then a warm wetness against her exposed wrist.

As she pulled herself clear, a great panting weight collapsed on her, and she realized Dusha was on top of her, covering every part of her face with licks.

"It's all right, Dush-Dush. Good girl."

Dusha's harness was still attached, but all Mila could see of the sleigh was a snapped-off wooden ring. She eased the dog off her and held on to the harness, and Dusha pulled her to her feet.

Mila swayed and blinked the world into focus. The snow crush had reduced the smooth side of the mountain to a choppy mess, and all about her were more peaks. It was still light, which meant she'd not been buried long.

She looked up behind them. There was no sign of the wolves; snow was still scattering from the shattered overhang, blocking the path through.

"Mila!"

Her heart filled suddenly at the sound of Pípa's voice, and she turned to see the small dark dot of her sister further down the slope, Danya sitting loyally by her side. Mila, choked with relief, threw herself downward, Dusha bounding along with her. Mila flung herself beside Pípa, holding her tight.

"Are you hurt?" she said, gripping her sister's shoulders and looking into her eyes for signs of the wide pupils that meant concussion.

Pípa shook her head. "Only a bit buried." She pointed to her leg, which was cut off at the knee by snow.

Mila began to dig her out, and Dusha joined in, sending snow flying, while Pípa chattered on. "I woke up and I was flying, Mila! And the mountain was falling, and I held on to Danya's harness, and he ran me clear. You weren't there, but I called and called and now you are."

"You should know better than to call after a snow crush," Mila scolded half-heartedly as she pulled her sister's leg free, and Pípa lay back as though making a snow bird. "You might've have set it off again. Where's Rune? Have you seen him?"

Pípa shook her head, suddenly tearful. "I couldn't see any of you. But the sleigh's over there." She pointed further up the slope. "That's where Dusha came from. She was digging there when you came out." She threw herself forward and hugged Mila painfully. "I'm really glad you're here, Mila."

She kissed the top of Pípa's head. "Me too. Let's go, Píp. I have to check the sleigh." She looked around and saw they were in a ravine, with a crown of mountains rising up on all sides. She felt a stab of guilt and glee: She was lucky to have avoided bringing the whole range down on their heads. Beyond them, yet more mountains stretched north in a long range.

"You go with Danya, up the side there, in case any more snow comes loose."

She helped Pípa to her feet, patted Danya, and waited for them to reach the ridge before she trudged back up toward the lump of the sleigh, pulling her fur cap back onto her head. It was slightly damp, but better than the funneled chill wind that had started to gnaw at her ears.

Dusha trotted alongside, trailing her broken harness. The snow was loose and dangerous beneath their feet, and Dusha was careful to stay beside Mila, so she could hold on to the dog when she sank too deep.

Finally, they reached the sleigh. It looked like a shipwreck—all their bundles scattered, clothes strewn like seaweed, planks of wood sprouting here and there. One of the rails stuck out of the snow at a right angle, like a mast.

It had flipped over completely, and Mila rubbed the soft spot at the base of Dusha's ears, glad that she had broken free. To be caught up in the wreck of the sleigh would probably have meant being crushed.

Rune. Mila could never forgive herself if her actions had hurt him. He'd helped them from the start, had been the only one to believe Mila about Oskar. What if this help and belief had cost him his life?

Dusha nuzzled her side, and then went to dig beside the sleigh again. Mila swallowed hard, kneeling to join her. The dog had already made good progress in the soft snow, and before long Mila felt the guardrail where the torches had been tied.

She felt along its length, left and right, scooping out the loose powder until the whole length of the sleigh was uncovered. She stuck her hand through the gap of the guardrail, and—

Something grabbed back.

"Mila?"

"Rune," said Mila, heart racing. "Give me my hand back!"

She felt relief and annoyance and rage all mushed up and boiling inside her. When Rune released her grip she smacked her hand on top of the upturned sleigh.

"Ow, that's loud!"

Mila banged it again. "Why did you give us the moonroot? Pípa could have been killed!"

"You're the one who started the snow crush!"

Mila chose to ignore this. "Yes, but she might have been hurt! And if I hadn't woken, we all could have been."

"And yet here you are, making a racket fit to deafen even those in the halls of the dead."

"Of all the stupid, unthinking—" She realized she was gasping for air, tears appearing sudden on her cheeks and powdering to frost. She collapsed in the snow beside the buried sleigh. "I could have killed her." She took a great, shuddering breath. "I could have killed you."

Rune's hand shot out of the gap and grabbed Mila's wrist again. "The wolves, Mila. You saved us from the wolves."

"But I didn't need to bring the mountain down."

Rune chuckled. "These mountains have withstood worse than a little snow crush."

"You're sure you're all right?" said Mila, relaxing her wrist into Rune's grasp.

"Yes," said Rune. "I'm sorry for scaring you, Mila, truly. And I'm glad you and Pípa are all right."

Mila could feel her eyes brimming and she wiped them hurriedly, glad the mage could not see. "I'm glad you are too."

"Mila?" Pípa's voice came thin and echoing over to them. "Why are you talking to the sleigh?"

Mila felt a laugh bubble up. "It's Rune, he's underneath."

"And he'd like to get out now," came the mage's muffled voice.

Mila led Dusha to the other side of the sleigh and tied her trailing harness to the guardrail.

"On my cue, curl up," said Mila. "We're going to flip the sleigh." She placed her hands underneath the rail and looked at Dusha, who stared back, tongue lolling, waiting for instruction. "Now! *Farash!*"

Dusha cantered away, Mila heaved upward, and the sleigh came off Rune in a great rush. He lay swirled like a sleeping dog. He really looked like a regular boy, Mila couldn't help but think.

"*Stuta!*" called Mila, and Dusha came to a stop as Mila helped Rune to his feet, letting go as soon as the boy was steady. Her relief that they were all unhurt was fading now that she saw what a state the sleigh was in. The sealskin bed was split in two, and one of the rails sat at a right angle to the sleigh. Heat flooded her numb cheeks. "Now what?"

Rune blinked at her.

"Now what?" she hissed again.

"We keep going." The mage frowned. "What else would we do?"

"The sleigh's ruined," said Mila bitterly.

"We don't need the sleigh." Rune started gathering their scattered belongings.

Mila looked down the slope, at Pípa throwing snowballs for Dusha and Danya to chase. The dogs were running full pelt after them, returning confused and empty-mouthed. It was a strangely peaceful scene, so different from minutes before. Mila shook, remembered the wolves' yellow teeth, their golden eyes, so like the Bear's. A sudden thought occurred to her.

"Rune?"

"Mmm?" He was packing another of his bags.

"How did the Bear know to bind the boy? To send the wolves? Does he . . . ?" A chill struck at her heart. "Does he know we're following?"

Rune looked up slowly. "I have been thinking the same. We can only hope he left them to make the route difficult for anyone taking it, rather than us specifically."

Mila did not feel reassured. "But the boy. He said my name."

Something flickered across Rune's face. He reached out and squeezed her arm. "We can't think on it, Mila. Not if you want to reach your brother."

Mila swallowed, and nodded. Another question forced its way out of her mouth. "Rune?"

"Mmm?"

"Why are you helping us?"

Rune sat back on his heels and smiled. His face creased up with wisdom that looked like it belonged to a much older man. Mila reminded herself that he was: that his herbs and magic were what kept him looking so young. There was so much about him she longed to know, to understand, but all her questions felt clumsy in the face of his moonlight eyes.

"Mila," he said gently. "How do you know it's not you helping me?"

"What do you mean?" she asked, confused.

"I mean that something has brought you here because there is something you must do. And it is the same for me." He held her gaze for a moment before breaking into a grin. "Besides, without you, I wouldn't have survived the wolves."

Mila felt a flush of pride. She held out her hand and helped Rune to his feet. "What is it you must do?"

"Are we going or not?" Pípa called, stamping her feet.

Mila jumped and looked around, raising her finger to her lips to shush her sister. "I warned her not to shout after a snow crush!" She turned back to Rune, but the mage was hastily gathering the last of his things.

"Rune, what must you—?"

"Pípa's right, we should get going."

Mila wanted to ask more, but there was a finality in Rune's tone that told her it would be hopeless to try to get more answers from him. Besides, there was no time. They had to get to Oskar.

She gathered what was most necessary—food, anything warm—and helped Rune wrench the broken rails from the sleigh.

Pípa trudged to meet them with the dogs, and Rune unearthed his parcel of food and gave them each a slice of black bread with flat, round seeds that Mila had never had before. On top he sprinkled flakes of flameberry.

She wrinkled her nose. "Do I have to have it?"

"Of course not," he said, "but it will help us make the journey faster."

Mila ate. It tasted a bit like moss, but in a good way.

After the meal, they wrapped their possessions in the ripped sealskin and Rune tied it onto his back. Mila and Rune lifted the rails parallel to each other, stopping them from sliding away with the bundled clothes.

The mage knelt and tied Pípa's boots to the detached rails first. Next he tied Mila's, and finally his own, so they were sharing the long rails like skis. They'd placed the dogs one in front of the other, and now Rune gave Mila the reins. Mila wrapped her arms around either side of Pípa and took a deep breath. *There must be no more delays*, she thought. *We must get to Oskar.*

"Ready?" said Rune.

"Ready!" cried Pípa, sounding so brave and definite that Mila felt a push of love rise in her chest. She squeezed her sister gently, then scanned the mountains ahead. She fixed the path in her sights and gripped the reins, the snapped leather squeaking against her gloves. She filled her lungs with freezing air. "Ready!"

CHAPTER EIGHTEEN

The Pass

Cold hovered like a carrion bird. The higher they went, the thinner the air, and it seemed to Mila the cold took on the shadowy presence of a crow, circling over her, finding her exposed wrists, the soft parts beneath her ears and at the base of her neck. It perched on her shoulders, making them heavy and stiff, dug needles of pain into her joints, buried its beak at her pulse points, cawed ice through her veins.

Mila saw now what a luxury a sleigh was, absorbing most of the unevenness of the ground. Now she felt each jolt of the rocky terrain. The wind moaned through her cap, crept up her nostrils and gummed into her eyes, making them stream hot tears that froze into gritty ice dust. The knots Rune had tied around her ankles bit tightly, and her legs felt sore and cramped from the slight bend needed to stop the jolts from shaking her knees out of place.

"Are you all right?" she asked, leaning forward to whisper to Pípa. Her little face was so bundled in furs that all Mila could see were her bright brown eyes, streaming like hers. Pípa nodded, and Mila twisted her head to speak out of the corner of her mouth to Rune.

"Will we ski through the night?"

"No choice," said the mage.

Mila drew the dogs back to a fast trot over the icy steps of the mountainside. The wind dropped a little here, nestled against the shoulder of the mountain, and Mila again looked up and up at its jagged teeth, wondering what it must be like to stand at the top and see all of the world stretched out beneath you.

"Have you been here before?" she called over her shoulder to Rune.

"Yes."

Mila sighed and turned forward again. *If he doesn't want to talk, I'm not going to force him.* But finally the mage seemed to relent. "I love the mountains. I love being up high."

She sent a shy smile back over her shoulder. "I'm not so sure about it."

"Nor me," said Pípa.

"I think I was a gyrfalcon once. Or perhaps I will be someday, in another life."

"You think you'll be a bird in another life?" Mila couldn't help but smile a little.

"My mother and grandmother became bird spirits," said Rune smoothly. "I suspect I will be no different."

"You really believe your family turned into birds when they died?" said Pípa.

Rune ignored her and tapped Mila's shoulder. "You're taking us too far to the west. The smoother course is further right."

Mila corrected the dogs and waited for Rune to reply, but he had fallen silent again. Mila let the silence stretch, focusing on the ascent. Finally, the dogs reached the summit and she pulled on the reins. "*Stuta.*"

She saw now that it was the way of mountains to carry on outdoing each other. Like in a forest, where the tallest trees vied for the sky—here the mountains seemed to graze on the sky itself. The mountain they had climbed now seemed more of a hill—and what faced them was a ridge barely wider than their skis. Mila thought she could see impressions in the snow, and thought of Oskar fighting through this biting wind. She flicked a look behind them, twisting as far as she could with her legs bound in place. At least the snow crush had stopped the wolves from following.

"Is that . . . north?" said Pípa, hesitantly.

The air felt even thinner here and Mila was struggling to breathe, though all she'd done was hold steady while the dogs labored. She shivered, and Rune squeezed her shoulder.

"Let's not delay. If we're lucky we can traverse it before sunset."

As soon as Mila started the dogs again, a wind hit them from the east, funneling through a gap in the peaks and smelling of wet stone and cold copper. It was a blunt wind, coming in one great slamming gust. They made themselves as small as possible as the dogs drew them forward.

She felt Dusha and Danya's uncertainty—their shoulders rolled lower to the ground, as if they wanted to slide along on their bellies. But Dusha was the braver, and soon her brother was matching her stride, drawing closer and closer to the cloud line.

Toward late afternoon a shadow split the snow before them, and Pípa gasped.

"Look up, Mila, look up!"

Mila tilted back her stiff neck. Above them shivered a shadowy shape. It seemed black against the gray clouds, but then it dipped and Mila saw two great wings, their span wider than her outstretched arms even at this distance, and then the twist of a feathered head.

"It's your mama, Rune!" laughed Pípa.

"That's too large for a gyrfalcon," said Rune, and his voice was tight, all knots where Pípa's was loose. "Too large for any natural bird."

Mila realized he was right. Though it looked like an eagle, it was vast: bigger than any she'd seen before, circling. Mila's stomach swooped as the bird did. And then the cords in her cloak began to warm, just as she'd feared they would. Mila felt them through her cloak, like a brand. The eagle's shadow crossed them—a great dark cloud—and grew bigger and bigger against the snow. Mila looked up just in time to see the eagle swooping closer. Its head tilted, and its eye glinted an otherworldly gold.

She thought of the bound boy. She thought of the wolves. *Bad things come in threes.*

"*Javoyt!*" A muttered curse came from Rune, and it pushed Mila into action.

"Heads down!" she cried. "*Farash!*"

The dogs shot forward so fast Mila had to almost bend double over Pípa.

"It's not a normal eagle, is it?" Pípa cried wildly. Mila's answer was muffled by her sister's hat, and she pulled her close, holding Pípa between her arms as they strained on the reins. Through streaming eyes she saw they were approaching the clouds, the incline leading them up to the sky. She was taking them blindly into it—there was no telling if the ridge veered left or right or fell off into nothingness.

The shadow, faint in the low light, circled again and again, growing all the time. Then, sudden as a gust of wind, it grew enormous, and Mila felt a rush against her face, heard a crack of wings beating, and Rune cried out in pain.

"Get away!"

A blow caught the back of Mila's head, hard as a punch, and she recled, seeing through bright spots of pain that the reins were loose and flapping, that the dogs were slowing and straying toward the ridge edge.

The eagle had attacked them! She grasped for the reins, but they whipped about her feet, and she could not reach them. She blinked hard, trying to steady her vision as Rune gasped and swore behind her.

But before she could get to her feet, the dogs were speeding up and running straight again.

"Faster, Danya! *Farash*, Dusha!"

Pípa!

Pípa had seized the reins and was urging them on, her high voice ringing out like a bell across the mountains, Papa's ring glinting on her thumb as she whipped the reins again and again. Mila wanted to reach for Oskar's knife but dared not let go of Pípa. If she shifted her weight too far, all of them would plunge off the ridge.

Again the eagle's shadow loomed to one side. It was wider than a man was tall, its beak a cruel curved dagger, its golden eye seeming to bore straight into Mila's body.

"Take the reins!" yelled Pípa, and Mila snapped her attention back to the ridge. She thought her sister was getting tired, and as she took the reins from Pípa's grasp she made to take over. But instead of leaning back into her, Pípa ducked down. For a moment, Mila thought she was falling, and almost dropped the reins again in the effort of snatching at her, but then she realized Pípa was fumbling with the ties at her ankles.

"What are you—"

The rest of her question was dashed from her as she felt the push of wind again on her cheek, and Rune forced her down. The eagle's talons scraped the back of her neck, shattering the cold numbness with bright hot pain.

As Mila ducked, Pípa straightened. She was holding tight to Mila to steady herself because she was no longer attached to the skis. Then her little sister was grasping for Oskar's blade, tucked into Mila's belt.

Mila could not spare the breath to ask for an explanation, and anyway, Pípa was moving too fast for Mila's mind to understand. Pípa swung herself around Mila's body, and Mila clenched her stomach to keep her balance. She scanned her periphery for the eagle, and saw it wheeling around again. Surely it would not miss them a third time?

She felt Pípa's light weight on her back, heard Rune grunt and felt his hands on her shoulders, braced there to support Pípa and lift her higher. Pípa was *climbing*, using them like a tree to get higher. And the eagle was drawing closer, its golden eyes fixed on Pípa, its vicious talons ready to grab—

"Píp!"

Mila felt the impact as the eagle snatched at Pípa. An inhuman scream tore through the air, and Mila felt fear swell larger in her belly. But then she realized the sound *was* inhuman—it was not Pípa, but the eagle.

And then the enormous shape was falling, falling, its wings in tatters, its talons snatching at nothing as it disappeared down, down, down. Mila felt Pípa's grip on her shoulders as she climbed off, felt Rune relax his grip. Relief flooded her limbs. She had to reach the top of the slope so the dogs could rest.

"*Farash!*" screamed Mila, and the dogs responded yet again. Up they rose, and up some more.

She gasped as they broke through the chill mist of the cloud bank. It was like hitting a foaming current. The cold seeped deep inside her, the way ice splits the cracks in rock and breaks them outwards. It seemed to lick around her very bones.

"*Stuta*," she whispered, and the dogs came to a panting stop. All three of them crouched down. Mila's thighs began to quake, and Rune placed gentle hands beneath her armpits to take her weight. All Mila could see was white, all she could hear was the black howl of the wind that brought the cloud swirling about them.

They stayed crouched down until Mila might have thought her body had turned to stone if it weren't for the pain radiating from the eagle's blow. Pípa was holding her breath, and Mila tightened her arms around her, burying her face in Pípa's scarf until she could feel her sister's pulse, beating as fast as a snared rabbit's.

Finally, Rune released his grip on Mila, pushing her gently up. In turn, Mila pushed Pípa, and they stood upright, calves cramping in their bindings.

"I th-think it's g-g-gone," said Pípa, a chatter in her teeth knocking the words loose. She held out Oskar's blade to Mila. It was stained with golden blood.

"Pípa," said Rune, wonder charging his voice like light. "You . . ."

"You saved us," said Mila. She replaced the blade in her belt and took her sister's cold face in her hands. "You saved our lives."

Pípa began to shake, and Mila longed to pick her up, hold her like a baby. She should never have brought her, never have allowed her to come on such a dangerous and uncertain journey.

"We have to move," said Rune, teeth chattering.

Mila bent to tie her sister's feet to the skis again. "Let go, Pípa. It's all right. You're okay. We're okay."

A fierce, bubbling anger swelled inside her. Pípa could have died. Somewhere, beyond the edge of possibility, their brother was bound in gold, trapped by a vengeful spirit. But there was no time to think on it, and she swallowed the bile down. They had to reach him. This could not all be for nothing.

She heard Sanna's sharp laugh in her head. *Yes, hurry up, Mila. Before the Bear steals our brother's soul. That's not wishful thinking at all, is it?*

Mila straightened, her spine clicking painfully, resolve tightening like a noose. *I'll save him, Sanna. You wait and see.*

CHAPTER NINETEEN

Bovnik

*T*he sun had been sinking fast before they entered the cloud, and all around them it was growing darker. Mila started the dogs again. Their tails lifted and they strained forward, the reins taut as fishing lines, making Mila glad for her thick gloves.

Finally, they broke the cloud cover. She looked all about them for the eagle, but there was no sign of it. The skies were empty above them: no birds, no clouds, nothing. What there was instead was a changed world. Pípa gave a whistle through her teeth.

"This . . . this . . ."

She stopped. There were no words for this. The sun was sinking to the west, staining the sky orange as firethorn berries. Before them was a sea of clouds, peaks of mountains marooned here and there beneath the endless, endless sky that was nothing like the sky Mila knew: twilight gray lightening at noon before folding them into dark again. This was a sunset full of color, though not warmth. And she had never seen, she realized now, the horizon.

But there it was. The edge of the world meeting some other edge, and the sun, sinking into it. And was that a break in the ice? An island, shimmering like frost on the northern horizon, hovering between this world and the next? Mila squinted, but the ice around them was bright and made her eyes smart.

"Is that Bovnik?" Pípa was pointing to the near distance. "Where Mama was from?"

Draped across twin peaks ahead, like the roots of a jeweled tree, were the sparse lights of the almost-abandoned city. Roofs glimmered in the sunset, and Mila remembered how Mama had told them it seemed the mountains pierced the sun at sunset and sent its light dripping down the buildings. And spun above it all was the trading platform Mama had once told her of that topped Bovnik, balanced like a playing card between the mountains.

"This is where the color hides," said Rune. His voice sounded weak and faraway. Mila remembered the blow of the eagle and wondered if it had caught Rune, too.

Bovnik grew brighter as the sun dropped. The city was built facing northwest, to enjoy the languid evenings of summers that had long since ceased to arrive. She could imagine the sun striking the city as Mama had said, coloring it gold and orange.

Ahead, a road was cut into the mountainside. Mila felt a flutter of nervousness at the sign of civilization. They had made it so far; they could not fail now, surely? The road was wide enough for two eight-dog sleighs to pass each other, and ski runnels were worn deep into glossed ice, making the going quick and smooth. As they came to a wide curve, the sun flooded the horizon and was gone all at once.

"Should we stop?" asked Mila. She didn't like the idea of continuing in the dark, however good the road.

"It's strange," said Rune. "The way should have been lit by now. Wait." She heard him rummaging for something. He pulled out a vial of brimstone and threw it at a trough set into the mountainside. The trough caught fire in both directions.

"How—?"

"Oil," said Rune, as Mila gasped and watched the fire spread around the mountain and out of sight. "Used

to be that the torchbearer lit it at sundown every night."
He sounded worried.

"Oil? They burned oil just for light?" She couldn't
imagine such a luxury used so frivolously.

"They had plenty of everything, before the winter,"
said Rune. "They thought such waste a good thing—an
impressive thing."

Mila could tell by Rune's tone that he was not
impressed at all. But she was. It was a waste—of course
it was—but it was also clever, and comforting, to have
light to navigate the road by.

"Have you been here before?"

"My spirit has."

Pípa gave a little snort. "Your spirit?"

"Mm. You know when you have dreams that you're
flying?"

"Yes."

"It's like that, except my spirit is actually flying."

"Or you're just dreaming," muttered Pípa, so quietly
only Mila could hear.

They curled around the mountain, below the houses
they had sighted from the ridge. Only a handful had
lights burning from their small round windows. The

houses were shaped like beehives, curving out from the mountainside.

"They're caves," explained Rune. "They're built out from the natural breaks in the rock. The curved walls stop the wind from taking hold and ripping them out."

Mila imagined huge hands raking the mountainside, reaching inside the hive-homes like a bear seeking honey. A chill slithered down the length of her body as she remembered the eagle plunging at them, as she remembered a deep voice speaking her name, and a hand reaching into her head and squeezing like a vise.

Finally they reached a set of gates, carved into the rock and lit by two huge torches. Mila pulled the dogs to a stop, untied her feet, and stepped from the skis. Rune copied her, and then moved to a grating in the rock that Mila had to squint to see, and reached through. They heard the sound of a lever being pulled, and then there was a creaking, grinding noise, as loud as thunder, and the gates began to open in the middle.

"You'd think they could spare some of that oil to grease the hinges," whispered Mila, and Pípa giggled, but Rune's face was grave as Mila knelt to untie Pípa's ankles.

"Leave these skis—we'll walk from here. You two stay quiet and stay close."

Mila released the dogs from their harnesses and they shook themselves, melted ice whipping off their fur. Dusha yawned, then came to stand beside her, while Danya went to Pípa.

"Good girl, Dush-Dush," murmured Mila, placing her hand on the dog's warm, soft head as they stepped into the city. Her legs were weak after all the skiing, and walking felt as strange as swimming. It was odd how quickly her body had adjusted to the crouch of skiing, to the thinner air.

"Where is everyone?" said Mila. The mountain was ridged and tiered. The tier they stood on was the widest, jutting out from the mountain on a ledge of rock. The houses looked even more like hives up close, their rounded walls as smooth as paper. The next, narrower tier overhung them by some fifty feet, and Mila saw it was made of wood, struts crisscrossing above them. But there was no one in sight.

"Many of them left when winter came," said Rune. Mila nodded. It made sense: Mama had told them how treacherous the mines were in winter.

"Or perhaps the Bear scared them away," said Pípa. "Did your spirit dreams not show you it was abandoned?"

"They did not," said Rune, seemingly missing the tease in her voice. "At least it makes going up easier— no one to ask questions."

Easier for the Bear, too, Mila thought as she craned her neck. "How do you get up?"

"There are steps," said Rune.

He started walking, but Mila hung back. She wasn't here for a tour.

"How is this the way to Thule?"

"You'll see," said Rune quietly. "Let's go."

CHAPTER TWENTY

The Climb

As they made their way to the steps, a few faces finally appeared, peering out at them through the windows. They were thin and furtive-eyed, looking away as soon as Mila turned her gaze on them. They were too busy surviving here, Mila supposed: No one was interested in them, nor even in a man the height and width of a bear.

The city brought a wave of homesickness crashing over her. She missed the forest, its trees; how even after Papa had left, there had always been the four of them. Four people who had promised to care for each other no matter what.

We must rescue Oskar, she thought fiercely. *Things must be as they were.*

They passed the open door of some stables, and when Mila peered inside she saw a dozen ponies drinking from a trough and eating from piles of frozen hay. One stood larger than all the rest, a horse with a black mane and tail.

"I think these are his!" Mila exclaimed. "The boys were on ponies. And he was on that one."

Rune doubled back to look in. "Probably. He takes what he needs, and leaves it when he no longer requires it. They'll be taken care of, though. There are still some people here. Probably too poor to get out." He looked around. "We should leave the dogs here too." Dusha was already sniffing and straining toward the trough. "There's plenty of food, and they can look after the bags while we climb."

Mila's hand tightened on Dusha's harness. She'd not thought about this parting, though of course they couldn't come to Thule.

"They will be safe here," said Rune gently.

Mila nodded and sank to her knees, wrapping her arms around Dusha's neck and breathing in her warm biscuity smell. "Be good, Dush-Dush."

Dusha whined in the back of her throat and nuzzled in deeper to Mila's embrace. Pípa hugged Danya, and then the sisters led their dogs to the trough. Rune began shedding bags, taking out vials and several strange orbs, placing them in a pouch attached to his belt until he clinked like a knife-sharpener. Like Geir.

"What're those?" asked Mila, pointing to the orbs. They looked a bit like soap bubbles, only with thicker outsides.

"Breath-skeins," said Rune, leaving Mila just as confused. She checked that she had Oskar's knife and the two pieces of golden cord in her cloak pockets before leaving her bag in the corner of the stable too.

Dusha and Danya were still drinking, and Rune pulled on her arm.

"Come now," he said softly. "While they're distracted. It's easier."

She nodded mutely and let herself be led away by Pípa while Rune shut the door. There was a tearing inside her chest. *With Dusha and Danya*, she thought, *it's like traveling with a piece of home. Now* . . . She tightened her grip on Pípa's hand.

They reached the steps, which were more like a ladder, a slice of lighter gray rock cut at foot-high intervals into the mountainside. The steps dipped slightly in the middle from years of use, and looked perilously slippery, though the torches burning alongside them were keeping them free of ice.

"Why do the platforms not catch fire?" asked Pípa.

Rune frowned at her. "What do you mean?"

Pípa pointed. "They're wooden. Isn't it dangerous to have the torches so close?"

"They're not wood. They're bone."

"No one has bones that big."

"Whales do," said Rune. "The largest ones are their ribs."

Mila's eyes widened. She could see now that the struts of the platform were curved, and overlaid crossways with smaller bones. *Whales.* Mama had told her they were huge, that one catch could feed and keep the torches of whole villages lit for weeks.

But still, Mila had never imagined something that had bones the size of trees inside them. She pictured something that large floating—*how massive the sea must be to have hundreds of whales in it!*—opening a mouth as wide as a ship, its tongue the size of a sail. It would render even Sanna speechless. She placed her hands on either side of her own chest. Even in her thick cloak and winter vest, her whole rib cage did not match the width of one of those bones.

"Time to climb," Rune said.

Mila's legs were sore from skiing, and she was overcome by the scale of the whalebones. She simply did not see how it would be done—the climb, the rescue—any of it. And to go up a mountain, to reach an island beyond imagining? Her head spun with the ridiculousness of it all.

She tried to focus on the movement of arm, then leg, then other arm, other leg, the pull and push of the slow ascent, her ragged breathing. *Don't look down.* Rune had brought them this far. If it weren't for him, Mila would still be in Stavgar, sure that Oskar had not left her willingly but uncertain how to follow him.

Finally they reached the trading platform. Mila's arms shook. No matter how deep she breathed, she could not take in enough air. Pípa looked in similar pain, clutching her ribs. The air was tangibly thinner, sharp with the salt of the sea, leaving her lungs gasping for more. Rune pulled himself gracefully over the top and stood, breathing steadily. He did not seem tired at all.

"We made it," he said, and Mila looked about them. The trading platform was empty, just a vast expanse over the empty maw of the mine. A strange creaking sound, a bit like the gates opening, wafted up to them, and Mila realized it was the sea, groaning under its cage of ice. There were no torches here, but they did not need them, because the sky was shot through with stars, more stars than she had ever seen.

The sky was actually glowing, not in the way it sometimes did with the sky fire, the colored flames that licked the sky on especially cold and clear nights, but as if the sun had been shattered and scattered into a thousand fragments. Here and there were sprinkles of stardust, fine as gossamer, stretched over the dazzle and shine.

At home Mila's view of the heavens was obscured by trees—slices of sky with trees overlaid like fingers over her eyes. But here it felt as if she were in a giant upended bowl, perforated with light. From horizon to horizon, she could see stars, and there, to what must be the north, something glassy shimmered. The frozen Boreal Sea. And was that the smudge of land she thought she had seen earlier, on the far-off horizon?

"Is that . . . ?"

Rune narrowed his pale eyes, more moon-like than ever in the crisp winter starlight. He seemed to freeze, only his breath betraying movement.

"Is that Thule?"

He nodded.

"How do we get to it?"

Rune pointed to a wide crevasse to their right, fenced off by a rope. Mila went and peered down.

And down.

And down.

She gripped the rope, her balance faltering as though she stood on a ship at sea, not solid rock. A waterfall was skimming down the mountainside facing the sea, and far, far below them a river was flowing beneath ice, white foam crashing against rocks, the water racing faster than Mila could run.

"A river?"

Mila traced the course of the river until it sliced out of sight into the night. North. To the Boreal Sea, choked to stillness with ice. And caught in its grip was an island, where her brother waited—she hoped.

"Don't we need a boat?" She stepped back unsteadily. "Do we have to break the ice? Why did we climb up?"

"We have to find the right current. The current the Bear placed there to reach Thule."

"The right current? How will we know it? How did he place it there?"

Rune smiled. "It's the Bear's favorite color. But you can only reach it if you have enough speed."

She eyed the waterfall, his words sinking in. "We have to jump?" The mage was untying his belt, head bowed. "Rune?"

He took five of the orbs from his pouch and attached them to the belt, then held it out. "*You* have to jump." Breath-skeins, he'd called them, and the name's meaning made its way uncomfortably into Mila's head.

Mila stared, uncomprehending. "You're . . . you're not coming?"

He wasn't looking at her.

"Rune, why aren't you coming?"

"Because I cannot," he said, finally raising his head to meet her eyes. His gaze was steady, full of sorrow. "You have to go on alone."

"She won't be alone," said Pípa, taking Mila's hand, but Mila shrugged her off, still staring at the mage.

"Why can't you come?"

Rune took a deep breath. "Because I would not survive it. You can only reach Thule once because you can only return once. A second time would mean death. And there is something I must do here."

"A second time?" Mila's mind reeled. "You've been there before?"

The mage swallowed, and nodded. Everything seemed to fall into place. That was why Rune knew the way, had been so confident in his ability to reach this island beyond imagining.

Mila realized, with a flash of wounded shock, that this must have been what he'd meant when he'd said all he could do was get them there. He could come no further. She felt a strange anger, but he looked so sad she could not help but reach out to him, resting a hand on his shoulder.

"Were you trying to save the boys?" Pípa asked. "The ones taken before?"

A strange, choking sound, halfway between a laugh and a sob, came from Rune's throat. He was staring at the ground as though he wanted to sink into it. "Pípa," he said. "We are not all so good as you."

"What do you mean?" Pípa frowned at Mila. "What does he mean?"

"I don't know," said Mila. "Rune?"

She drew closer to him, sliding her hand around his shoulders. He jerked away.

"Don't. I don't deserve your kindness."

An icicle of foreboding pierced Mila's heart. "What did you do?"

Finally, he met her gaze. His silver-white eyes were full of tears. He sighed, and began to speak.

CHAPTER TWENTY-ONE

Rune's Tale

"We have little time, so I'll make it brief. When I was young—truly young, not only in appearance but in my spirit—my mother still lived. She was admired throughout the land, all through the forest and beyond for her magic, her knowledge of herbs and readings of fate. I have some power, but my mother had more in her little finger than I do in my whole soul.

"I should have been proud of her, I see that now. But I was jealous. I wanted the respect she had, the power. And so when she told me of the Bear, the once-powerful guardian of the forest, I thought I had found a way to prove myself. I thought I could defeat him, and take his place. I thought I could be a ruler, of sorts."

He hung his head. "How wrong I was. I stole my mother's books, learned the way to Thule. I faced none of the dangers we have, and only now am I understanding why—I was no threat to the Bear."

"You couldn't defeat him?" said Pípa, eyes wide with tension.

"Obviously," said Mila sharply, irritated by the interruption. "We're here, aren't we?"

"I never had a hope. If I had paid more attention to my mother's warnings, I would know there is no way of killing the Bear on Thule. He must be drawn away from the place, for he feeds off its magic."

"He can't be killed?" asked Mila.

Rune shook his head. "Not there. I crossed into Thule, and faced the Bear. But my vials were of no use. I wasn't even able to *attempt* to free the boys I found there before alerting him to my presence. I was foolish, arrogant. If my mother had not followed me, bargained with the Bear to grant me safe passage, I would have died on that island."

"What did your mother bargain with?" asked Mila, her voice barely above a whisper. "What did she give?"

Pain flickered across Rune's face. He seemed unable to speak, and pulled the words onto his tongue with great effort. "Her life."

Pípa gasped. "Oh, Rune!"

"Do not pity me," he snapped. "It was my arrogance that killed her, my need for respect. And in trying to earn it, I lost the one person who cared for me."

He wiped his eyes fiercely. "But Thule's rules are not the only reason I can't come. There is something I must do here." He shook his head. "I would be no help, anyway."

"No help? Rune, you brought us here," said Mila.

"Thule changes to fit the person arriving there. For me, it was a mountain pass; for you, who knows? More importantly, you will have a better chance of saving your brother if I am not there."

"How can that be?" Mila felt abandoned, hopeless, and Rune clasped her hand. His was warm, and anchored her.

"You may succeed where I failed because you care, Mila. You care about your brother—the forest."

"So do I," said Pípa sulkily. Rune laughed softly.

"And you, of course. But I failed because my heart was not true. I did not care for those poor boys, not truly. I did not even care for the forest. I cared only for the praise, the glory that would come with being the guardian of the forest, with defeating the Bear. I wanted people to love me." He glanced up at Mila and Pípa. "People like you."

"But we do love you, Rune," said Pípa, reaching out to him. He smiled sadly.

"And I love you. That's why I could not have you go to Thule without understanding why I can't help you further. Because I want what I did wrong all those years ago to be made right, and I'm sorry it falls on you."

A sharp wave of hurt flooded Mila's chest. "Not because you want to help us? Not because we're your friends?"

Rune blinked, tears falling down his anguished face. "Of course that too."

"Stop being silly, Mila," said Pípa.

Mila bit back a retort. Pípa was right, but it didn't stop Mila from feeling angry. Angry at Rune for not ending this years ago, for not telling them this tale at the start. How was she supposed to face this without him?

Still, she did not move away when Rune stepped forward and looped the belt of breath-skeins around her waist. She stared dumbly down at his hands as they buckled it, listened to his gentle words: "Listen, Mila— these are all the things you will need. When you enter the waterfall, use the breath-skeins. Then, when you reach Thule . . ."

Mila heard Rune through the rising buzz of blood in her ears. She did not want to do this without him.

She could not do this without him. As he described what they would find in Thule—strange and terrible things—she wanted to scream, to shout at him and shake him until he agreed to not make them face them alone. But if he came, he would die. She could not ask him to sacrifice his life for her, though she was certain, now, that she would for him.

"Do you understand, Mila?" He was standing very close to her, still smelling of apple smoke and herbs. He took her hands gently. "Repeat it back to me."

But at that moment she felt a warmth begin to pulse at her side and she gasped, pulling away from the mage. She placed her hand in the pocket of her cloak and felt, confusedly, that the cords were warm. *Not now*, Mila thought, flashing on the frozen figure, the wolves, the eagle. *Not now, when we're so close.* She drew one out. It glowed.

Rune and Mila locked eyes, fear reflected in them as Pípa stepped toward the stone steps, eyes wide with shock.

"Sanna!"

CHAPTER TWENTY-TWO

The Drop

Mila wheeled around, certain Pípa must be mistaken, or seeing things. But there, hauling herself over the final stone step, dressed in her blue dress and fur-trimmed cloak clasped by Geir's brooch, was their eldest sister. She stood up and looked straight at Mila. Her face was thunderclouds and lashing rain.

"Sanna!" called Pípa again.

Mila took a step back even as Pípa rushed forward to clutch Sanna's skirts. Sanna did not hug her back, only stood there, inscrutable, eyes clamped on Mila. Mila felt a creeping unease.

"At last we've found you." Their sister's voice held no celebration. It was smooth and gray-solemn as a river stone.

"We?" Pípa frowned. A moment later, another figure stepped onto the platform, and Mila gazed into the stern face of the jarl.

"Hello, Rune," said Bretta. "What a merry chase you have led us on."

"We led you on no chase," said Rune. "We didn't ask you to follow."

Mila thought of the eagle, the wolves: She thought they had thrown off all their pursuers, but here were yet more.

"What else is a jarl to do when she discovers two of her youngest wards have disappeared with her most dangerous?"

"He's not dangerous!" protested Pípa.

"You left no word, Mila." Sanna's accusation flashed like lightning. "Not even the ring, like Oskar did. And you took that, too."

"I took it," said Pípa, holding up her thumb. "It's as much mine as it is yours."

"I had no choice but to leave," said Mila, pleading. "You didn't believe that Oskar had been taken."

"Because he hasn't!" Sanna's chest heaved. "He is *gone*, Mila. Gone because he couldn't stand his life with us. A life you make so hard—"

Bretta held out an arm and Sanna fell silent, as though slapped. "As you can see," Bretta said coldly, "you have worried your sister nearly to death." There was a definite threat in the woman's voice, and Mila felt the hair on her arms rise, as though she'd been plunged into an icy bath.

"How did you find us?" said Rune suspiciously. "How did you catch up?"

"We rode through the days and nights. Bretta saw how important it was to me that we reached you quickly." Sanna's voice had a reverential tone that made Mila's skin crawl.

"How did your dogs manage that, Bretta?"

"Seems you're not the only one who knows their herbs, mage." The jarl wore an almost wolfish expression, a snarl. Her body was tense as she approached, though when she saw Mila watching her, she loosened her stance, rolled her shoulders back.

"Come now, child. Away from the mage."

"He's our friend," said Mila.

"Why are you *here*, Mila, of all places?" said Sanna. "I thought you said you never wanted to leave the forest?"

"I told you. I had to follow Oskar."

"He's here? In Bovnik?"

"No." Mila hesitated. "He's north. In Thule. Right there."

She pointed at the horizon, but the stars had been covered by cloud and the sea was suddenly dark and quiet, with no island in sight. There was a silence fit for a funeral.

Bretta laughed, a little too loudly. "Thule?"

Mila ignored Bretta and spoke only to Sanna, trying to make her understand. "I know it sounds mad—"

"Someone has been telling tales." The dangerous edge was back in Bretta's voice, and her eyes were fixed on a point behind Mila. On Rune. "What nonsense have you been filling these girls' heads with, mage?"

"It's not nonsense," said Rune. "The Bear took them to Thule. And it's not too late to get them back."

"Shut up," said Bretta bluntly. "Why should we believe you? I should have thrown you to the cold a long time ago."

"It's the truth," said Rune. "Mila has seen him for what he is."

"I have," she said. "I told you, Sanna: His feet didn't sink in the snow. And when he spoke my name my head ached."

"Why must you always think you're special?" spat Sanna. *"That's* why you think he's Eldbjørn? He's not, Mila! He's just a rich trader who convinced a bunch of pitiful poor boys that he knows the path to treasure. That's all. It's pathetic, that you'd believe this boy just because he tells you you're Oskar's only hope."

"Enough, children," hissed Bretta. "We are returning you to your home. Come, now." She reached out and took Mila's wrist in an iron grip.

"It's not home without Oskar!"

"You're wasting our time," said Bretta. "I've left my people in their time of need to fetch you. I can delay my return no further."

"Don't you want the boys back?"

Bretta laughed hollowly as she began to drag Mila back to the stone steps, back down the mountain. Mila tried to wrench herself away, but it was like fighting a current. A moment later, Rune was there, trying to separate them.

"Let her go!"

Bretta shoved him, and Rune grabbed her cloak to steady himself. It ripped slightly, and beneath it something glinted.

Bretta hurried to readjust her cloak, but it was too late. Mila had seen what was wrapped tight around the woman's wrist.

Gold cord.

"He has you, too." Mila's voice seemed to cause the wind to dip.

She looked from Bretta's face to Rune's to Sanna's, then pulled out one of the glowing cords from her cloak. The jarl scowled, a muscle feathering in her jaw, then she let out an unnatural shout of laughter. "What?"

"You've made a pact with the Bear." Mila took hold of the rip in Bretta's cloak and pulled, revealing the woman's arms. The cord laced her wrist to the elbow, tied so tight the skin pushed up through the gaps, shining with the same strange pulse as the cord in her own hand.

"What do you mean, made a pact with a bear?" Sanna's voice was skeptical. But her eyes were wide, and she looked back and forth between the jarl and her sister.

Mila ignored her, eyes fixed on Bretta. The tendons in the jarl's neck tensed as she fixed her jaw, baring her teeth.

"Come to me, Pípa," said Mila, and Pípa edged toward her. Mila stepped in front of her sister, pushing her as far away from the jarl as possible.

"That's how you knew where to find us," said Rune. "That's how you caught up to us. Like the boy, the wolves, the eagle . . . *he* sent you."

Mila felt as though she were at the still point in a storm. Everything slowed down and she could hear only a roaring in her ears, the blood punching through her body. She looked down again at the cord.

"What's that?" asked Sanna.

Bretta glanced at Mila's hand, and Mila could have sworn her eyes flashed, just like the wolves'. She hurriedly looped the cord over her belt as Rune placed himself between the jarl and Mila, talking in a low, calming voice, as though to a wounded animal.

"I know you had no choice, Bretta. But you can fight him now. I can help you—"

Bretta howled and was suddenly running, surging forward, straight toward Rune. The mage sidestepped her and wrenched Mila out of the way, but he was too late to save them all.

The jarl's momentum carried Pípa over the edge of the waterfall.

Sanna screamed.

"Pípa!" Mila rushed forward and threw herself onto her belly, hands reaching uselessly as the two figures pitched down and down. Pípa must have fought because suddenly Bretta spun away from her and hit the slick, icy rock. Mila felt a moment of pity, that the Bear's control had claimed another victim. But her thoughts rushed instantly back to her sister.

A moment later, Pípa plunged directly into the churning water.

A terrible, snake-like fear reared up in Mila, baring its needle-sharp teeth, but she used it to make steel of herself. She made herself deaf to Rune and her screaming sister, and she stumbled to her feet.

She looked toward the waterfall. Toward the black roar and freezing mist. Toward the impossible, iced-over drop.

And jumped.

PART 3

Thule

CHAPTER TWENTY-THREE

The Golden Current

$\mathcal{M}$ ila cursed herself as she fell. She had always known she was not a particularly brave person, so why did she keep doing brave things? Even now, as she felt her body fly and then fall, she did not want to look. She squeezed her eyes shut, thought of Bretta on the ice, and knew she was going to die.

She could not open her eyes now even if she wanted to. They were gummed together by tears and cold, and the force of her fall blurred everything even behind her lids. Her stomach felt as though she'd left it on the platform when she jumped.

Distantly, she thought she heard Sanna scream her name, but the sound was ripped away by the rush of wind and the gush of water. She felt the chill of water as her clothes skimmed the waterfall, felt her cloak grow heavy with it, felt the wind slapping her cheeks and ripping the cap from her head. She did not want to stop feeling.

She wished she'd started counting to have some idea of how close to the bottom she was—but as soon as she thought this she felt icy water clap its hand over her feet.

Mila inhaled sharply, and the next moment she was fully beneath the water. It was as shocking as a slap. Her brain itself seemed to freeze, the water rushing through her cloak so fast she might as well have been naked with anchors tied to every limb. She felt no hint of the current Rune had promised, only a great, crushing pressure on her shoulders and back. She forced her eyes open. Freezing water clung to her eyeballs, boring a sharp needle into her temples as she grasped about her, searching for Pípa in the mouthing blackness.

Panic, dark and cloying as oil, spread through her body. Her cloak wrapped about her arms and legs, and she struggled out of it, but it was hopeless. Her lungs began to ache. Bright spots appeared in the black panic. She was going to drown. Where was Pípa?

There!

Ahead through the dark water she saw a pale figure. They swam toward each other, and suddenly Pípa's hand was in hers, her other scrabbling at her waist.

Of course! Mila had nearly forgotten. She wrenched two orbs from the belt, and the girls placed them in their mouths.

What do I do now? But before she could decide whether to swallow or chew, Mila's teeth caught on the orb and burst it, like the skin of a berry. Inside was not fruit flesh, or liquid, but air. Air that tasted like damp moss and dew. Like home, before the winter.

She sucked it down, and the effect was instantaneous. Though her head still spun, the explosions faded to distant stars. Pípa pointed downward. Mila's eyes were wide open now, her body so numb the water felt almost warm, and she knew that this was when the cold was most dangerous—when you stopped feeling it. Still, where Pípa was pointing, something appeared to be glowing.

A thread of light, green and gold and bright as the sky fire, wove in and around the water at the bottom, playful as an otter. But other lights were joining it, the stars in her vision spreading into explosions again, her chest desperate for breath. She brought another orb up to her mouth, letting the air dissolve slowly through the skin into her mouth, giving her a longer breath.

They were almost down to the bright current now, the gold like a seam running through water that was otherwise black as wet stone. Mila didn't know how they'd be able to tell which direction was which without the light of the golden thread dancing along the bottom of the river. She kept a tight hold of Pípa and let the water push them to the bottom.

Finally, Mila's fingertips brushed the golden current, and—

She was wrenched forward, as though caught on a hook or the tip of a wind spin, torn from Pípa's grasp. A moment later she felt her sister's hand close on her ankle.

The gold thread appeared to be a length of fast-flowing water that swallowed her whole and pulled her along with it. Her ears popped as she hurtled along, this time desperate to keep her eyes open but barely able to. All she could discern was the gold-green shimmer weaving around her. Pípa's grip felt like the only solid thing in the whole world.

Somewhere there must be rocks, she thought frantically, but they hit nothing, only shot forward. Was this even water? It felt like wind, wind all around them, cocooning them. It was hard to believe they were below anything, that somewhere above them was the river, and above that the ice, and above that the stretch of the ravine, and finally the sky, so huge and star-filled.

It felt impossible that her body could travel so fast, so perhaps it wasn't possible. An image came to Mila suddenly of Rune laying his hands one over the other and telling her about realms overlapped like fish scales. Perhaps they were slipping through one realm to another. Perhaps she had been pulled from herself, and it was her spirit left now in the golden light, on its way to the other world.

The orb of air was dissolved completely now, leaving only the lingering taste of an early forest. Mila tried to sip at the rest of the breath, but her heart was beating too fast, her fear swallowing air like fire does, sucking it bodily from her mouth.

Just as the stars punctured her vision again, just as the darkness began to swallow the edges of light—the golden seam spat them out.

Mila landed hard on her back, and the breath she'd sucked in only moments before was wrenched back out. Winded, she gasped and writhed onto her side. Beneath her gloves, the ground was springy like moss, and when she managed to open her eyes, she saw that that was exactly what it was. She pushed herself up, her lungs slowly filling again, and blinked out at the world as Pípa landed with a thump beside her.

"That was far worse than I'd imagined," wheezed Mila, massaging her neck. "And I thought I'd imagined the worst."

"At least Rune gave us those. . . ." Pípa was panting. "What were they again?"

"Breath-skeins." Mila hurt, an all-over ache radiating along her back and across her chest, shooting down her legs and pulsing at the back of her head. And under it all sat a different hurt: that Rune wasn't there.

If it weren't for the pain, she would have thought she'd left her body behind in the underwater sky fire. Papa had always said that's what the afterlife must feel like: like coming home. And it was as if she *were* at home in Eldbjørn Forest again, the trees familiar, the smell comforting. Except the forest was different in one vital way: there was no snow, no ice. Trees in green leaf spread out above them. Rune's voice floated to her. *You must find the way past winter. . . .*

"Is . . . is this . . . ?" Pípa's voice was full of wonder.

Mila swallowed down a sudden lump in her throat. "Spring."

CHAPTER TWENTY-FOUR

The Compass

Mila had forgotten it was possible for the ground to feel like this, for there to be so much green in the world. If someone had asked her just yesterday, she would have said she didn't recall what moss felt like, and yet now that she was in it, she remembered. Her body remembered. They were in a birch grove, and apart from the lack of a heart-tree it felt exactly like the one she used to visit with her family all those years ago. She ran a hand over the moss, remembering how her bare feet would sink into it, remembering Mama's hand in hers. . . .

There was no sign of the river that had spat them out, only a trickle of water emerging from a gap in a small cairn of rocks, right where, in their home grove, the heart-tree stood. It seemed impossible that they had emerged from there. Where was Bovnik? Above them, no mountains, no snow—just a blue sky filled with light, but no sign of the sun, and all about them were bright green trees and warm air. It was spring, but wrong, somehow. Unnatural. The mage's song rose unbidden to her, even in this place of spring. *It knows your fears, and it knows your name.* She shuddered despite the warmth.

"How did we get through there?" Pípa asked, eyeing the cairn, her voice echoing in Mila's popped and sore ears. But as they watched, the edges of the water began to ripple, as though they were a reflection in a windswept lake. Mila frowned and pulled at her sister's arm, pulling her backward, further up the hillock. They moved just in time.

The next moment, a body was thrown onto the moss below them, raven-black hair slick and stuck to her cheeks. Mila gasped and crawled forward.

"How did she—?" started Pípa, but Mila's eyes were locked on their elder sister. Not even her chest moved. She was not breathing.

"Sanna!" She moved her sister's hair away from her mouth. Her cheeks were pale, her eyes half-closed. Mila's stomach churned as she brought her ear to Sanna's chest. A faint heartbeat stirred beneath her sister's ribs, and Mila thought of whalebones, big enough to hold up a city.

"The breath-skein!" Pípa's exclamation pierced her panic, and suddenly her little sister was scrabbling at Mila's belt for the last remaining orb. She wrenched open Sanna's jaw and pushed it inside. Mila kept her ear on her sister's sodden winter vest, wishing the whisper into a drumbeat.

"Come on, San," murmured Pípa, and, as if she'd heard her, Sanna's body gave a great shudder.

Then Mila took Sanna's shoulder and rolled her onto her side, and it seemed as if she'd had the whole river in her lungs, so much water came out.

Mila rubbed her between her shoulder blades, feeling the heartbeat beneath her palm thump steadily. *Thank the stars!* When Sanna had stopped vomiting, Pípa threw herself at both sisters, squeezed them so tight Mila felt she might be the one to have trouble breathing next.

"You're hurting us, Píp," said a muffled Sanna, and their little sister's grip relaxed. "What just happened? The water—it was gold." Her voice was still thick with water. "And where are we?" She sat up carefully. "Is this . . . home? Oh, but—the trees—they have leaves!"

"This is Thule," said Mila. "It's where the Bear brought Oskar."

Sanna raised an eyebrow at her. Mila raised one back. "Just look around, Sanna. It's spring."

Alongside mingled wonder and fear, Mila felt the fizz of anger in her belly. The Bear had taken spring from her forest and brought it here. He had doomed them to an eternal winter, stolen her brother and brought him here—and why? For what?

Sanna's arms came up. Mila flinched, but instead of pushing or pinching her, Sanna held her almost as tightly as Pípa had done. Mila leaned into the hug, inhaling the cold river smell of her big sister, listening to her breathing. It was the best sound ever made.

Which reminded her—now that she listened for other sounds, she heard none. The forest was deathly silent. A prickle of fear went up Mila's back. She pushed gently away and looked around. "We need to get moving."

"How do you know which way to go?" Sanna asked.

"The same as always," said Pípa confidently. "North."

"Which is . . . ?"

Mila blinked around them. It was warm, but there was no sun, and anyway, she didn't know if time worked the same way on Thule. "We can make a compass, like Papa taught us."

Sanna frowned at her. "You remember that?"

"I wasn't *that* young," said Mila, upending the pouch Rune had filled. There were three vials of brimstone, and small pots of flameberry and moonroot.

"What're those?"

"Rune gave them to us," Mila replied, the mage's name sticking in her throat. "We can use this for the water." She tipped out the moonroot and handed her sister the empty pot. "Pípa, will you fill this?"

Pípa went to the cairn with its trickle of water while Mila sifted through the vials and pots. "We need a needle, something metal."

Sanna, who had been staring at her, rubbed her face. "A needle, yes. I . . ." She looked down at her sopping dress. "I have this."

She tenderly touched Geir's brooch, then took it off, letting her cloak fall to the ground. She wrung out her dress. "This will soon dry."

Mila hesitated, placing her hand on Sanna's. She knew how much the brooch meant to her. "I'll have to break it."

Sanna swallowed, then set her jaw and snapped off the back of the brooch. She held it out to Mila with a faint smile, though her eyes shone. "If you're right about this wild quest, he'll be able to make me another."

Mila took it gently and began to push the pin through the fur trim of Sanna's fallen cloak in long strokes, as if she were trying to wipe it dry. *One, two, three . . .*

Pípa brought back the pot of water and set it on the mossy surface. "What're you—?"

"Hush, Píp," said Sanna softly. "You'll make her lose count."

Once Mila reached one hundred, she carefully lowered the brooch pin into the water. It caught on the surface and slowly, strangely, began to spin—once, twice, and back onto itself, until it finally settled. Mila squinted down at it, then looked in the direction the point was indicating, past where Pípa sat.

She followed it with a finger. "That's north."

"How—?" began Pípa.

"Currents," said Mila, removing the pin and emptying the water. Sanna held out the broken brooch, motioning for Mila to put it in her pouch.

"Currents?"

"Like the sky fire," said Sanna.

Pípa frowned. "The northern lights?"

"Mmm," said Sanna, helping Mila gather the scattered vials. "You know how they dance? It's actually more of a fight, between the sun's light and our air. Currents bring them crashing together. The needle is drawn north by the same currents."

"I didn't know that's how it worked," said Mila. "Papa always said it was magic."

"It is, of a sort." Sanna stood up and wrung out her hair. "We'd better get moving."

"Sanna." Mila hesitated. "The way it's telling us. That's . . ."

Sanna glanced at Pípa, but she was halfway up a tree, swinging from a branch. "I know."

"Don't you think it's strange?"

Sanna gave her an odd look. "Not the strangest thing I've seen today, if I'm honest."

Mila smiled, but uneasiness rocked her belly. The needle was pointing steadfastly through the trees, the trees that looked just like the ones she had grown up around. Pointing directly at the route that would, if they truly were back in their forest, take them home.

CHAPTER TWENTY-FIVE

The Familiar Forest

*I*t was good to be walking, but the shift from deepest winter to the warmth of spring was hard to adjust to. Mila shed her clothes down to her winter vest, and they all took off their woolen socks. The fur-lined boots made Mila's feet itch, but at least they were not so hot anymore.

"You must believe it now, Sanna," said Mila as Pípa ran ahead to shinny up trees and jump down again, laughing at the leaves that dropped with her. "In Thule, and the Bear? Now that we're here?"

"I don't really have a choice, do I? I was in the golden river just like you."

"And that Oskar was taken?" pressed Mila.

"I don't know." Sanna's face was downturned and shadowed. "An island of eternal spring . . . why *wouldn't* he want to come here?"

"Why do you keep thinking the worst of him?"

"Because!" exclaimed Sanna. "Because of Papa. People leave. Even Ma—" She stopped herself, and flicked a glance at Pípa, who was halfway up an oak tree.

"Mama had no choice," said Mila. "And Papa—"

"Did," said Sanna cooly. "People aren't always happy with small lives. Perhaps we weren't enough for Oskar."

"He didn't think he had a small life," said Mila hotly. "Just because you hate us—"

"She doesn't hate us," said Pípa, dropping down as they passed beneath the oak. "Do you?"

"Of course not. I only wish . . ." Sanna fell silent a moment, and Mila listened to their feet and skirts rustling over the mossy ground, and to the greater, all-swallowing quiet of the forest.

"The journey," said Sanna finally. "I was furious with you, and worried sick, but didn't it make you see, Mila? See that the world is so big and so full of wonderful things?"

"So is home," said Mila sulkily.

Sanna's face was alight with excitement. "Those mountains, the sunset. I'd never seen a sunset that went all the way to the horizon. I've always been hemmed in by trees. The world is so large, and we live in such a small part of it."

Mila could think of nothing to say to that. They walked on in silence under the endless trees.

"How much further?" grumbled Pípa after a while.

"Not sure, Píp. I've never been to an island of stilled spring before, have you?" teased Sanna, but she cast Mila a look that meant she thought she knew exactly how long—at least, if their suspicions were right and the path was taking them to where their house should be. Mila regarded her eldest sibling. Sanna had tucked her skirts up between her legs and tied them together, making baggy pantaloons. She looked sort of dashing, her raven-black hair now dry and slicked back off her face, but Mila would never have told her that. She ran a hand through her own curls and her fingers immediately got snagged on an egg-sized knot.

Mila felt an unpleasant sort of wakefulness, as though her eyelids were held open by matchsticks and her skin was tingling with buzzing insects. Rune had told her a little of what to expect, but still, she knew nothing was certain.

Mila kept her gaze fixed on the moss beneath their feet, the itch of her winter vest a welcome distraction from her racing mind.

"There!" Pípa suddenly exclaimed, pointing. Sanna gasped.

Mila raised her head. She had to blink several times to be sure of what she was seeing.

A dome rose in the center of a clearing, a clearing that looked exactly like where their home was located. But there were no dog sheds, and no building of wood and moss, with a chimney belching smoke. Instead, there was this dome. This *cave.*

Mila peered closer, and saw that all about it, where the land around their home was bare and scuffed, there were wildflowers—purple and red and blue—rippling like wheat in a breeze. They were the flowers that used to bloom around the heart-tree in spring, but here they grew so thick and so high Mila felt sure they were magic. The cave looked like an island, marooned in a calm, colorful sea. It glittered white, like marble.

"What's that?" asked Sanna.

"The Bear's cave," breathed Mila.

"Is that where Oskar is?"

Mila nodded grimly. She realized that until now, she had forgotten to be afraid. Walking through the forest had felt comforting, like being at home, even though in Eldbjørn Forest the trees were weighted with snow and the river was caught under a pane of ice, thumb-thick. Here, walking through a spring forest, it was easy to forget that this island was not on any map. Now Mila looked behind and the trees seemed to be straining after them.

"Come on," she said, moving clear of the treeline and into the field of wildflowers. The sisters stepped forward.

When they'd viewed it from the forest, the cave had seemed to be no more than half a mile from the trees, but every time Mila stood on tiptoe to see over the head-high grass and flowers, it was as though it had drifted slightly further away, like a lazily tethered cloud. The scent of the wildflowers was overpowering, and all she wanted to do was lie down amid the whispering grasses and sleep. She imagined Oskar approaching the cave. Had he been afraid, or so deep under the Bear's spell that he hadn't felt or seen anything? She didn't know which would be worse: fear or oblivion.

Eventually the cave loomed over them, and she felt a dizzying sense that it might topple and fall down, smashing them to pieces. She shuddered, and tried to calm her hammering heart, which was throwing itself at her ribs like a caged bird.

The flowers grew up to a line of low black stones, beyond which was a raked stone path and the curve of the cave. Mila stopped at the line. Maybe the stones would turn into a thousand scuttling crabs and nip them to pieces, or the path would suck them in like sinking sand.

Pípa had no such worries. She crossed the line as if it were nothing.

"Come on," she said impatiently. Mila and Sanna followed. The wall of the cave was dazzling up close, too bright, and Mila shaded her eyes. It seemed smooth and impenetrable, without weakness.

"How do we get through?" said Sanna.

Mila closed the distance between them and the wall, and after a moment's hesitation held out her hand

and placed it gently on the rock. She had the strangest sensation that if she pushed hard enough, she could push all the way through. Like dough.

What had Rune said when she first met him? Something about feeling with more than her fingers, seeing with more than her eyes . . .

"Come," she said to her sisters. "We have to push through."

Sanna snorted. "That's impossible."

"Isn't this all impossible?" snapped Mila. Her head was starting to throb, her legs to ache. And every second, time was rushing by. Oskar was moving closer to . . . not death. What Rune had told her about the fate of the boys was almost worse.

She forced herself to speak calmly. "Please, Sanna. Try to see. Try to feel. It's not rock at all. Watch."

Mila closed her eyes and took a shaky breath, repeating Rune's words to herself: *There are things in the world that you have to look at with more than your eyes, hear with more than your ears, touch with more than your fingers.*

She had seen the Bear stand on soft snow and not sink. She had seen a boy bound by the ice, watched wolves and an eagle and a jarl attack them with other-worldly fury. She had seen her brother's face become that of another.

She had seen all these things, and now she knew she could see the wall for what it was. Dough it felt like, and dough it would become.

Mila pressed softly. She was in the kitchen with Sanna, watching her plunge her fingers into the flour sack and bring them up with a flourish, scattering a thin dusting on the wood of their table, the table where they'd carved their given names into its soft underside. She held a cup of fresh-melted snow, and watched her sister scoop a double handful of flour onto the dusted tabletop, sift it through her fingers and form it into a mound. She made a hollow with her thumb and nodded, and Mila began to pour the water into the hollow, a little at a time, pausing for Sanna to work the water into the flour.

"What're you doing?"

Pípa's voice came as a shock in the quiet of Mila's mind kitchen, but Sanna shushed their little sister and soon Mila was back, watching as the flour and water performed their small alchemy. When the dough was formed, it was Mila's job to leave it by the fire to rise, and she imagined reaching down to press her palm into it. The dough was warm and flour-dusted, firm but not solid. She pushed a little harder, feeling it give, taking her hand in, pushing up between her fingers.

"How are you doing that?" There was wonder in Sanna's voice, and Mila, careful not to lose the sensation of the dough, opened her eyes.

Her hand was embedded in the wall.

Mila's heart began to beat faster, and she swallowed down the panic that instantly rose at the strangeness of it. Because what she felt turned into what she saw. Her story was coming true: The wall was less solid now, the marble turned to glittering ice crystals held in a cloud, and she was pushing through it.

"How—?"

"Shush, Pípa!"

Trying to ignore her sisters, Mila focused on the movement of her hand, sinking deeper until she was in past her wrist. She allowed herself to breathe more regularly, and brought her other hand up, pressing it alongside until she was up to her elbows and her nose was touching the—what?

Mila stopped, breathing so close and hot a small hollow was forming at her lips, melting the wall and sending water trickling down her arms.

"Is that snow?"

This time Pípa shushed Sanna, and Mila saw and felt that that was exactly what it was. It was an enormous bank of snow, swept up high as a hill to form the formidable walls of the cave. It did not make sense: The blue sky still shone with sunless light; behind them the field of flowers waved their heads lazily. But she was up to her shoulders in snow. Her arms began to burn with the cold shock of it.

"Are your hands through?"

Mila shook her head. It was thicker than her arms' reach.

"Now what?" she said in a small voice, mostly to herself. But Sanna came to stand beside her.

"We will all push through at the same time. Run, and keep on running. Whatever's there."

Mila felt a small match of hope strike in her thudding chest. Sanna, finally, seemed to be on her side.

"You have to believe it's snow," said Mila. "Believe it, and you'll see."

"We'll believe," said Sanna. "We'll make it true. Ready?" Pípa and Mila nodded. It felt good to let their big sister boss them around again. "Three, two, one!"

Mila stepped inside the snow. The sounds of her sisters disappeared, muffled to silence. It was like being back in the snow crush, but this time she had solid ground beneath her feet.

Using her arms as paddles, she swept the snow apart, straining her legs against the compacting, trying not to listen to the creak and pop that meant the balance of the wall was shifting above them. It was strange how much compact ice could sound like wood in a fire.

After five tortuous strides, her hands found air. Mila leaned forward, using her elbows to draw herself out of the bank, and tumbled face-first, down into the Bear's cave.

CHAPTER TWENTY-SIX

The Grove of Souls

*I*nside was dark as dirt, dark as a grave. The hole they'd made was high above them, leaking meager light, the slope of the ground cushioning her fall. Mila heard Pípa and Sanna collapse beside her, and instantly groped for their hands, holding them tightly in the blackness. She stretched her eyes as wide as she could, the sudden cold of the cave making them water.

Mila knelt, still holding her sisters' hands, shuffling them closer together. She could hear only their three sets of shallow, fearful breaths, feel only the blunt shunt of darkness pressing in. Beneath her knees was what smelled like the bitter richness of earth.

She unfurled her hand from Sanna's, who let out a small mew of fear and reached down to touch the ground. It was dirt, but mixed with something. Mila flinched as her hand traced a gnarled shape.

Wood—roots twisting across the floor. She sensed Pípa and Sanna also reaching down, and felt a sudden heat at her side. She thrust her hand into her cloak, knowing already what she would find. . . .

The two pieces of cord shining gold, as hot as sunbeams in her hand. She gathered up her cloak to hold them.

"Those again? What are they for?" whispered Sanna, her voice terribly loud in the yawning silence, her face lit by the eerie golden glow.

"His," replied Mila. "They're what he uses to bind the boys."

"Why do you have them?" hissed Sanna, looking as though they were snakes coiled to strike.

"I . . . we . . . found them." Mila could not bear to recount the story of the second piece.

"At least we have a light," said Pípa.

There was only one way to go. The tunnel stretched before them, roots catching the paltry light, paving the path ahead. Toward Oskar. Toward the Bear.

Heart thrumming in her chest, palms sweating, Mila took a step, and then another. She paused between each one, listening. But the earth muffled their steps so well that had she not looked back at regular intervals to make sure they were still together, she might have thought herself alone. Pípa's face was drawn in the thin light, and Sanna walked beside her in her torn and ragged skirts, biting her lip.

The tunnel seemed to go on forever, the light and heat from the gold cords growing stronger and stronger, until eventually Mila saw a flickering ahead, as though from a fire. Sanna froze.

"Milenka," she murmured. "I'm afraid."

Mila squeezed her hand. "Me too." It felt good not to be alone in her fear. "Come. Oskar's waiting."

They hugged the shadows of the black walls, and approached the light. The ground dropped suddenly away. Mila flung out an arm to stop Pípa from charging ahead. Before them was a cavernous space, reaching as deep below them as it did high above. At its center was the most fantastical thing Mila had ever seen.

"What . . . ?" breathed Sanna.

Mila swallowed. "His heart-tree."

It was at least ten times bigger than the one in Eldbjørn Forest, even at its most majestic height. It arrowed up before them, its base a tangle of body-thick roots, its trunk so colossal ten people with their arms outstretched could not have encompassed it. And growing from its massive branches were leaves as large as sails. They were gold, like the cords in her hand, and cast everything in a flame-like light, stronger even than the torches ranged about the room, though no sun shone on any of it. The light seemed to come from inside the tree itself.

Mila could see no sign of the huge, broad figure of the Bear. But what she could see was almost as awful.

There were dozens, perhaps hundreds, of smaller shadows: Tiny trees twisted into bizarre shapes, leaning toward the birch at their center. Each was bound with gold cord that snaked its way to the base of the heart-tree, disappearing into the snarl of roots.

Perhaps it was merely the glitter of the tree and torches casting everything in a tricky glow, but Mila could have sworn the cord was pulsing. Even the pieces of cord in Mila's hand seemed to twitch. She shuddered and pushed them back into her cloak.

"What are we waiting for?" said Sanna, suddenly bold. "Where's Oskar?"

Mila felt sick as she remembered what Rune had told her at the top of Bovnik's waterfall. It had felt so impossible she'd hardly believed it. But now she had to tell her sister where—or rather *what*—Oskar was.

"He's somewhere there," said Pípa weakly, stretching out a trembling finger. "That's right, isn't it, Mila? That's what Rune said."

Sanna squinted at where Pípa was pointing. "Behind the trees?"

Mila shook her head carefully, her gut churning. "They *are* the trees."

Sanna could have been turned to ice, she froze so completely. Only her lips moved, trembling. "You . . . you mean . . . ?"

Mila took her sister's hand once more. She spoke as clearly and calmly as she could, trying to recall what Rune told them: "He turns them into trees. He plants them, to feed his heart-tree. See how some are still more boy than branch?"

Sanna peered more closely at the shapes. Mila tried not to look, but she had already seen—how some were only rooted about their ankles by gold cord, swaying as though in a breeze. Others were so enveloped in bark that she would not have known them from trees.

"Oskar—is he . . . what if he's . . . ?"

"That's why Rune brought us so quickly," said Mila. "So we could still get him out."

They looked down at the grove of planted boys, at the heart-tree rooted at their center. Mila wanted to weep, looking at the caught shapes.

"Can't we help them all?" asked Pípa, but sadly, as though she already knew the answer.

Sanna shook her head. "We're here for Oskar. We can't risk anything more."

Mila knew what it cost her to say that. Geir was down here too.

"Then let's go," said Pípa. Before either of them could stop her, she darted toward the steps that led down into the cavern. Sanna followed close, and after a brief pause, Mila hauled her courage into her chest and descended.

A few of the shapes that were more boy than tree looked up, but their movements were lackadaisical, like animals emerging from hibernation. Where was the Bear? In the snarl of roots? In the glittering leaves above? The idea that he might be watching them was almost worse than being certain of it.

At the base of the steps, Mila gestured for Sanna and Pípa to go right, and she circled left, trying to avoid touching any trees.

The shimmering light of the golden-leafed tree made them seem gilded: living statues meant to decorate the cave of the Bear. She tried not to think of them as people—as brothers or sons with homes and lives that might continue if they escaped.

Mila jumped. She felt breath on her cheek. A boy was speaking close to her ear, eyes unfocused.

"I'm sorry—" she began, but he wasn't looking at her, or talking to her, but to something in the distance.

She hoped that whatever the Bear did to keep them—*how had Rune put it?*—sunken into themselves, he allowed them to think happy things. Though, having met him, Mila doubted it. She backed away, bumping into another boy. She turned—and gasped.

CHAPTER TWENTY-SEVEN

The Rooted Boys

*I*t was Geir, reddish hair burnished to copper in the tree light, his cheeks sallow, his jaw slack. His hands hung limp at his sides, and his feet were bound with gold, sunk inches into the dirt.

Mila's throat tightened. She reached out and grasped his hand. It was rigid and rough as bark.

"Geir?"

The boy did not move and his expression did not change, but his eyes dragged themselves away from the middle distance to Mila's face. She swallowed and moved a little closer.

"Geir?"

His eyes looked like two black tunnels, their faded light growing sharper the longer he looked at her. She fumbled in Rune's pouch and drew out the brooch he had made Sanna. *Something he loved.* She held the two pieces up to his face, hesitated a moment, then placed the piece of elk horn in Geir's hand. The boy's fingers twitched, then brushed over the carved brooch. Mila held her breath, watching his face. Something slid behind his gaze.

Mila could not think what it was, but it was something alive, similar to the shadow she had seen in Oskar's face the night he'd been taken, only where that had been dark and eel-like, this was light.

Geir was coming back to himself.

A vein in his forehead began to pulse, and his eyes grew wide even as the light returned to them.

"Help me!" he gasped.

Fear was growing in his eyes, sucking his cheeks pale, filling his lungs with a scream that Mila did her best to smother.

"Hush!" she whispered fervently, holding her hand over his mouth. "Hush! He'll hear!"

But she saw she had made a terrible mistake. She had reminded Geir of who he was—and where he was. He pawed weakly at her hand on his mouth and was unable to move his legs, but she could see his mind was racing.

"Geir," she said quietly, as though talking to Dusha when she was frightened. "It's all right, Geir. I'm here, and so are Pípa and Sanna and—"

At the mention of Sanna's name, Geir's eyes widened. He looked desolate, desperate tears streaking his cheeks. Mila carried on talking, as gently and soothingly as she could, all the while looking about her for the Bear. Would he be able to tell when one of his prisoners had been woken?

"I had to break the brooch, you see? She'll be angry, so I need to return it to her mended. You can mend it, can't you? But you have to calm down, Geir. You have to promise not to make a sound. Do you understand me?"

She looked him in the eyes, and he saw her. He inhaled through his nose, and Mila pulled her hands from his lips.

She knelt and looked for knots in the cord where she could untie him, but there were none. It seemed to loop in one continuous, unbroken length from ankle to knee. She would have to cut it. Mila pulled Oskar's knife from her belt. Holding her breath, she worked it beneath the cord, and sliced upward.

The cord would not break. Mila tried again and again, but she could not cut it. The cord seemed to be made of something harder than metal. "I'm sorry, I can't—"

But Geir was not listening. He seemed frozen, looking behind her. Mila wheeled around, coiling her body, ready to run, or attack, but it was not the Bear.

Sanna stood there, eyes filling with tears. She stumbled forward, and Mila looked away as Sanna and Geir embraced. A moment later Sanna turned to her. "We found him," she whispered.

A shot of energy pierced Mila's body.

"Where?"

Sanna pointed. "I'll stay with Geir."

Mila hurried through the grove, casting a look at the heart-tree, her breath hitching as she thought she saw a movement in the uppermost branches, but perhaps it was only the golden leaves glinting. Ahead, Pípa came into sight, crouched next to a familiar figure.

Oskar.

Pípa was pulling at his cords, her shoulders shaking. Mila ran faster and at last looked into her brother's face.

He was thin and horribly pale, his eyes more black than brown, empty and staring. His feet were stuck deep in the soil, but when Mila brushed his legs with her fingers, they were still flesh and bone, not wood. He was there. He was alive. Mila felt winded. She wanted to throw her arms around him and never let go.

"There's no way to untie him!" Pípa cried.

Mila could see her sister's hands were blistered, and that the golden cord seemed to be tightening even as she continued to pull on it. Pípa had removed Papa's ring; Mila could see where the heated band had burned a welt on the base of her sister's thumb.

Mila pulled Pípa's sore hands gently away and once again tried to use Oskar's knife to slice through the cord, but it would not break. She hissed in frustration, then remembered how Geir's face had changed when she'd placed the brooch in his hands. *Something he used and loved.* She pressed the knife against Oskar's unmoving palm.

Oskar's eyes began to warm. He came up slower than Geir, less fearful, and she watched his mouth slip into the shape of her name. "Mila?"

"Oskar."

She at last held her brother again, beneath this monstrous tree at the end of the world. A smaller set of arms wrapped around her, and she felt Pípa nestle in beside them. The thunder of her heartbeat finally started to calm as Oskar hugged them back.

They let go. His face was still pale, but his eyes were bright with tears. "How . . . ?"

"There's no time," she said, looking around them. "We have to get you free."

"We brought your ring, Oskar," said Pípa, handing it to him as Mila knelt by his feet, trying to find a break in the cord. "I looked after it for you."

"You should keep it."

Pípa gingerly touched her burned thumb, looking at the ring with distaste. "I think Mila should have it. She's the one who made us come after you."

Mila jumped as Oskar gently slid the ring onto her middle finger. His hand, no longer stiff and dead-feeling but warm and soft after a week without chopping wood or holding reins, reached out and brushed her cheek.

The gentleness somehow made her feel every hurt in her body: from her sore legs to her bruised ribs, her aching feet and cord-burned hands. She wanted to let him lift her, as Papa used to, and carry her home.

But there was still so far to go. They had not yet learned how to break the cord. Rune must have thought Oskar's knife would be enough. If he was wrong about that, what else was he wrong about?

Even as this thought reverberated in her head, Oskar's careful touch tightened and then she was pulled from his grasp. He grabbed at her, but she was caught beneath the armpits, and in a horrible fulfilment of her wish was lifted as though she were small again and her father were scooping her onto his shoulders. But there were no hands beneath her, only her brother's panicked face and an awful expanse of cold wind that raised her high off the ground, and spun her to face the tree.

CHAPTER TWENTY-EIGHT

Caught

$\mathcal{F}$rom the snarl of dark at the mighty birch's roots came a figure. It was huge and shaped like a bear, but formed of . . . nothing. Where it should have had boundaries were rips in the fabric of the air, swallowing light. Limbs flickered in and out of being, like shadows only barely remembering to hold their form. A smell like bitter, rotting leaves clawed up Mila's nose, thick and biting as fanged smoke.

Her stomach filled with bile. She wanted to look away, but her eyelids were pinned open by the wind that was lifting her. Her ears popped as though she had been submerged deep into the golden current of the waterfall again—and then she heard his voice.

"You dare to come uninvited to my home? To try to steal my souls and destroy my new forest?" Mila was being held at the height of his eyes, many feet off the ground, and he was solidifying, forming into a bear with thick, shaggy fur and burning golden eyes. Over one mighty rolling shoulder, Mila saw the glint of his axe.

She felt a click in her throat, as if it had been released from a tightening noose, and her voice garbled out, pulled like a tailor pulling thread from yarn.

"You came uninvited to *our* home. And stole our brother!" She did not want to speak, but she felt she had no choice. She was conscious of her words yet somehow unable to control them.

He was really solid now, huge and stinking of forest rot. But though his paws were wide as tree trunks, his body mighty as a boat's hull, he drifted through the boy-trees with smoke-like ease. They seemed to shudder and bend away from him, cringing as though caught in a fierce wind. His eyes fixed her in his awful, animal gaze. "Ah, yes. Little Mila."

She cried out as his voice bore sharply into her head. It felt as though his use of her name was a blade, scraping off her skin and making her nerves shimmer with pain.

"You saw me without my cords."

Through the haze of agony, Mila remembered his unbound feet, hovering above soft snow. They were unbound now, too. *The cord must contain his magic,* Mila thought, *bind him fully into his human form, just as it binds the boys' will to his own.*

"Very careless of me," the Bear roar-hissed. "But girls are often disarming. That's why I usually do not bother with them." The Bear's face twisted in a dreadful smile, yellow teeth showing in the swallowing dark of his face. "But I'll make an exception today."

Below her, she saw a flash of blue dress. She tried to stop herself from looking down, but it was too late—the golden eyes followed her gaze, and a slow terror filled Mila's body as his jaw opened again, another baring of teeth cracking the black fur of his face.

"I almost forgot there were more of you. Do we have the complete set? Sanna, wasn't it?" Mila heard a thin keen of pain from her sister, and felt another rush of cold wind as Sanna was wrenched from her hiding place and raised up to hover beside Mila. She tried to reach out to comfort her sister, but her arms were trapped against her sides.

"I hope Pípa is here too?"

Mila's breath caught as she fought the impulse to answer him. There was silence.

"Pípaaaa," he crooned, but all was still and quiet. Mila's mind raced. She had to keep him talking.

"Why do you take the boys?" she cried. "Why did you send the winter?"

He stopped casting around the grove and fixed her in his golden gaze. "Who told you I sent the winter?"

Now Mila's mouth turned traitorous. "Rune!"

The glinting eyes flashed in recognition. "The boy-mage. Did he not tell you this is a fool's errand?" He smirked. "I murdered his mother, you know."

She flinched with his casual mention of the slaughter of Rune's mother. "Well?" she said, more bravely than she felt. "Why did you take them? Why did you bring the winter? You have ruined lives, you're killing my home—"

The Bear stood on his hind legs, bringing himself tall as a tree, and roared. It was half-howl, half-sob: pain and anger circling each other like wolves. The sound slammed through her body as Mila felt the supporting wind ripped from under her. She landed hard on her back at Oskar's rooted feet, and he cried, "Mila!" Beside her, Sanna landed too, moaning in pain and reaching out for her, trying to shield her. Pípa was still nowhere to be seen.

The Bear bounded forward, threw Sanna aside with one massive shoulder and bore down on Mila, filling her vision until his awful face was all she could see, his reeking breath all she could feel, his words all she could hear.

"*Your* home?" he spat in his howling voice, with such force the boy-trees around them shook and Mila's hair blew off her face. "The forest was never your home. It was *mine*. Humans brought nothing, planted nothing, and took everything." His eyes were wild, wide with hurt. "*I punish those who threaten that most sacred place.*"

Her heart quaking in her chest, his body bearing down like a wave upon her, Mila remembered the heart-tree lying dead and broken on the forest floor. She knew what it meant to call the forest home.

The Bear gave a snarl and threw himself off her, sank back on his haunches, the blade of his wood-cutter's axe toy-small against his bulk.

"Five years ago, that man"—he spat the words like they were a curse—"chopped my heart-tree to pieces like it was nothing. He tried to kill me, kill my forest. So I brought what I could save of the heart-tree to Thule. I planted it here, so it would always be safe and strong." He looked up at the birch with pride and love, and Mila followed his gaze. The vertiginous trunk made her head spin.

"Someone chopped down your tree?" Mila said. "Why? Who?"

"I never cared to ask." The Bear's gold eyes glinted at the trunk. "But I planted him the deepest."

Mila gasped. About halfway up was a shape, larger than most of the others, twisted with bark but still, just barely, recognizably a man, melded with the massive trunk and held so thickly with golden cord it was like a fly had been wrapped by a giant spider. The hurt in the Bear's eyes hardened into fury.

"He tried to kill my heart-tree, so—I made him the new heart. I keep this tree strong with the very people who would make my forest weak: the men who never stop chopping it down. I feed it on souls and spring, and I will take every boy of Eldbjørn and keep endless winter there until you are all dead or gone. Then I will return to *my* home, and bring spring with me to the forest once more."

Mila saw his fur begin to bristle. His anger was barely in check: Soon he would lose control entirely. She hurried to say something, anything, to calm him.

"That's a terrible thing, a cruel thing," she said, as soothingly as she could with her voice shaking. "But why have you done something so cruel and terrible in return? Why punish all boys for one man's crime?"

The Bear looked at her. His eyes were wary as a fox's in a trap. "Because boys grow into men. And without men in the forest—a forest of eternal winter—in time there will be no more people. Soon I will have driven every—last—one—of—you—out." He pounded the ground with each word.

Mila's teeth rattled, and she was thrown back against Oskar's legs. It was a shock to feel him behind her, still rooted in place.

"Now, Mila. Didn't I say I always welcome those who come, tired, to my door?" The Bear reached down to where the roots were shining golden at his paws. He brought his axe to the root, hooked the edge of the blade through it, and pulled.

Mila gasped as the root began to stretch, lengthening like it was not wood at all, but something pliable, like dough. *Like half-dried sap*, she thought, remembering the mess of the frozen heart-tree, honey-red sap caught like blood falling from a wound. *Like a cord.* He stretched the cord until he had a length the height of him, then sliced it into two pieces with his axe.

The Bear crouched over the root he had pulled it from, which was ragged and pulsing along the ground, and placed a huge paw over it. His golden eyes closed a moment, and Mila saw him slump slightly. His paw was light on the root, almost tender. When he took it away again, the root was smooth, running in an unblemished twist to the trunk of the massive heart-tree. He had healed where he had severed it.

The tenderness vanished quick as a finger snap when he looked up again. "Enough for you both," he said in a smile-snarl of a voice. "Mila, Sanna. Bind yourselves."

He threw the cords down, and to Mila's horror, her first reaction was to reach for a piece. Her shoulder nearly wrenched out of its socket in her haste to pick it up. She couldn't stop herself, and she knew now how the bound boy back in the woods had felt, how impossible it was to resist the Bear's commands. Sanna's arm shot forward too as his words repeated themselves in Mila's head, so loudly it crowded out her own thoughts.

Bind yourself. Bind yourself. Mila tried to resist, and felt Sanna struggling beside her.

"Now, girls," came the Bear's voice, warningly. "If you fight, I will break your mind. You'll die not knowing who you are, that you were ever loved, without a memory in your head. So I think you'd be wise to do as I say."

Mila fought her grasping hands. *Bind yourself.* Her will broke, and his voice rushed in.

And so did Pípa.

CHAPTER TWENTY-NINE

The Heart-Tree's Heart

It happened in a moment. Pípa's small, swift shape leapt from the shadows of a nearby tree, through the air and onto the Bear's back. Mila saw her land lightly on his shoulder. He turned his massive head, and at the same time, the Bear's voice in Mila's head broke off. Release!

Sanna threw down her cord and tore Mila's piece from her hands. The Bear let out another roar, reaching to his shoulder for his axe—

But Pípa was too quick. All her practice climbing trees on even the most blustery winter nights had given her a grip of steel, and she already had the axe in her grasp. She shimmied off the Bear and darted toward her sisters.

"Come here, Pípa—" he snarled, reaching for her, but Pípa did not so much as flinch. He had no power over her. *Of course!* Mila realized. *She doesn't have her given name!*

The Bear's form began to shift and ripple. He was turning into a spirit again. Once he did, there would be no trapping him. Through her panic Mila remembered bound legs sinking into snow. . . .

She unfroze. "Wrap his legs!" she yelled at Sanna, who picked up the fallen cords. They ran forward together, Mila yanking the other pieces from her cloak and leaping up to bind the arm that swiped at Pípa. She caught it and brought the ends of the cord together. Instantly they sealed, tightening around the Bear's arm just as Sanna trapped each of his legs.

The Bear howled and keeled forward like a felled tree. He was bound on both arms and both legs, his shape shrinking and sharpening its edges, back into a man, the stranger who had come to their door all those nights ago. Mila threw herself clear and Oskar bent to her, still caught at his ankles, and dragged her to her feet.

Though he was trapped in his man's form, the Bear was still as unrelenting and deadly as a snowstorm.

He pulled himself up and toward Sanna, who was brandishing Oskar's knife.

"His axe!" cried Mila. "Give me his axe!"

She watched the glinting arc of it fly from Pípa's hand to hers, felt an awful, tearing pain as the blade grazed her palm. Her mind went numb, not letting her feel the damage as she fumbled for the handle, already slippery with blood, transferring it to her other hand. It felt familiar in her grasp. Now, she was certain.

"You're hurt," started Oskar, but she did not listen.

She bent and sliced through her brother's bindings. Then she turned from him and began to run.

The Bear's words were like wolves, snapping at her heels. *Five years ago, that man chopped my heart-tree to pieces.*

Five years . . .

Mila fixed her gaze on the bulge in the trunk and ran toward it, ignoring the fire of her injured hand. At the base of the tree she tucked the axe into her belt, ripped a section of her skirt with her teeth, and, trying not to faint at the sight of so much blood, wrapped it twice around her injured hand. It wouldn't stop the pain, but at least it might stop the bleeding.

And now she could climb.

Mila looked at the shape sealed in the tree. It was higher than Mila had ever climbed, even before Papa had left, back when she used to climb trees. It was a good thirty feet before the lowermost branches began.

You mustn't think of it like that, said Papa's voice. *It's only one hand after another, until you reach the top. One hand at a time.*

Mila dropped her gaze, scanned the bark, and found her first foothold. The trunk was oddly warm. It reminded her of the cord, its vague pulse. She placed one foot into a twist of root, and pushed herself up. She reached with her injured hand, biting down hard on her lip, letting the pain rush over her. *One hand after another.* Mila began to climb.

The rhythm of her reaching, pulling, pushing, matched the sickening twin pulse of her heart and hand. Her limbs felt like lead, her skin raw, but she would not let go.

She heard the Bear snarl. "Mila!" He was hurtling toward the tree in human form, cord shining around his limbs.

He was fast, but Mila knew she could be faster. She would reach the heart-tree's heart. And she would rip it out.

Her anger propelled her better than fear. Before she knew it, she was hauling herself on to the branch below the gold-webbed shape, and instantly began to slice the axe through cord after cord, letting them shrivel and fall.

At last the tree's bark was revealed. Without hesitating, Mila plunged the axe into it. She heaved it downward with both hands, her injured palm aflame with pain. The bark was thick as sea ice, but it gave way beneath the blade. Once it was split, she tore great hunks of it away and pressed her hand against the smooth wood beneath.

It was pale and pulpy, softened and ringed with years. But it was not shaped like broken wood. There, that was a chest, a man's chest, dressed in a brown tunic. And that was a hand, snarled into woody knots, but a hand still. And here was a face, eyes black whorls of wood, a face she knew. . . .

The pain in her hand, the roaring of the Bear, the screams of her sisters: It all dropped away.

"Papa."

Mila stared, wondering, at her father's carven face. It felt as though she were underwater, her body moving through thick currents, dragging her down.

She knew what she had to do.

She pulled the ring—his ring—off her finger, where Oskar had placed it. She brought it up to the gnarled hand. She slipped it over one wooden finger.

Nothing happened.

Mila pressed the ring harder against the tree, holding it in place as she leaned her forehead on her father's still chest. Was that a flutter, faint as a moth throwing itself against an ice window? Tears came streaming hot down her cheeks as she cradled her cut hand and whispered, "Come back, Papa. Come back."

Pain in her hand was all that answered. She felt it now, and it bit and stung and throbbed, wrapping her whole arm in thorns. She had been so sure she was right, so sure it would work.

Beneath her clutching hand, the ringed finger twitched.

Boom. Boom. Boom.

A far-off knocking in her ear, growing louder and louder until finally, the chest beneath her head heaved. Mila's father blinked his eyes, now ice-blue, then keeled forward, pulling them both out of the tree—falling.

Mila could not think what to do but hold on. They were hurtling down, her father as limp as a corpse. With a sickening thud, they hit a branch that broke their fall, Mila shielded from the worst of the impact by her father's body.

He let out a cry of pain, but to Mila it was as wonderful as a laugh.

"Papa!" She flung her arms over him.

"Mila?" his voice was wheezy and dry as firewood. His eyes fluttered open, struggled to focus. "My Milenka?"

"Mila." The Bear stood on a branch above them. Terror gripped Mila's throat as her name in his mouth sent pain grinding through her skull. "Give me back my heart." The Bear was panting, his fingernails torn and bleeding. His golden eyes flashed. Mila stood between him and her father.

"And drop the axe," he hissed, pointing with his bound arm. "Or I will throw you off this tree."

Mila moved the axe—her father's axe—behind her back, even as her mind urged her to hand it over. The pain in her palm was becoming stronger, stinging like a hundred bees. She could see the cord glowing around the Bear's limbs, forming an unbroken circle. He was trapped fully in his human form, but he was still as dangerous as a caged animal.

Mila shook her head, the coin taste of fear rising as her hand pulsed. She dared not look at him directly.

"Very well," the Bear snarled, coiling himself to leap, when the heart-tree gave a yawning creak. Mila and the Bear both looked up at the place where Mila had carved her father out of the trunk.

The tree creaked again, then swayed. Suddenly, with an awesome *crack*, the trunk split above their heads, and the entire canopy began to tip downward.

The Bear roared, and it was the saddest, most frightening sound Mila had ever heard. It was pain and anger and fear, all mixed together in one mighty sound that filled her whole body.

Her world tilted as her father threw her over his shoulder and swung himself down on to the tree's trunk. She could barely believe he was real, but here he was, holding her, his body warm and his grip fierce.

"Hold on, Milenka!"

The Bear fell silent. He seemed shocked into stillness, could only watch as his heart-tree came tilting, almost slowly, lazily, toward the ground. Mila lost sight of him as her father swung them down, branch by branch. But she could not lose sight of what was happening to the tree, or what was coming from it.

The bark was blackening, as if it were smoldering, and the whole cavern was filling with light. When Mila felt heat, she knew it must be fire . . . but she could smell no smoke, hear no crackling flames.

Instead, a mossy, green scent was filling her nostrils. A scent she had almost forgotten before they had arrived in Thule, but now remembered as birds in trees, and flowers underfoot. It was the smell of the whole world stretching itself awake.

It smelled like spring.

Mila's hand was hurting badly, a nauseating, rhythmic stabbing that came in time with her heartbeat. She felt herself fading as she hugged it to her, keeping a tight hold on her father's tunic with the other. Her fingers found the darned patch that Mama had mended, sitting beside the kitchen fire. Mila had been no more than four, had played with the dangling thread. She heard her mother, round with Pípa, laughing. . . .

And now she could hear Sanna crying "Papa!" and Oskar saying "Run!" and more shattering creaks, and the smell of spring was growing stronger and stronger.

All around them were moans and cries, and Mila saw the whole grove was swaying, as though caught in a breeze. The golden cords were fading, turning black, like the bark of the heart-tree. It was dying, and the Bear's power was dying with it. The boys were waking, remembering themselves, struggling free of the charred bark, branches reforming into limbs and chests and terrified faces.

Mila thought she felt rain, and, looking up, she saw the snow dome of the cave was melting. The freed spring bathed everything in a light so bright it clawed at her eyes.

She shut them again, and felt Oskar take her in his arms, and, through half-closed lids, saw Papa being supported by Geir and Sanna, Pípa running alongside. The whole cave was shaking as the tree gave up its roots.

But where is the Bear?

"It's going to come down on our heads!" yelled Oskar to the waking boys. "Get out! Run!"

Now Mila smelled burning. It felt so out of place she did not instantly recognize it, but when she turned toward the felled tree she saw a dazzling brightness as the released spring sun caught the dead trunk in its jaws and began to devour it, flames leaping faster and higher with each passing second. The heart-tree burned as the cave dissolved, and the sky was suddenly pressing down on them with a fierce heat.

"Hurry!" shouted Pípa, and they followed her, up the steps and into the burning air, a girl too young still for her given name, yet she was like a jarl leading her troops to battle.

Oskar set Mila down gently, panting hard, supporting her as best he could, though he swayed with weakness.

Mila looked around. She could see no trace of the tunnel, or the forest they had walked through. The field of wildflowers was fading before their eyes, replaced by land that was barren and dead-looking, and Mila could see the sea was quite close—the island had become far smaller than it had seemed when they'd traversed it on their way to the Bear's cave. Spring had been released, and Thule seemed to be dying.

Or maybe it was just showing its true form, how it was before the Bear had come.

Beyond the island's edge, beyond the sea caught beneath its winter ice, was land: Bovnik, with its shining slice of thawing waterfall.

But now there was a new danger. A crack like a whip sounded from somewhere beyond Mila's sight, and Sanna gasped.

"The ice!" she shouted. "It's melting!"

CHAPTER THIRTY

Across the Frozen Sea

Oskar hauled Mila into a run. Every breath in her chest was like a vise being screwed tighter and tighter, allowing less and less air, but she kept her eyes on Oskar, and on her father just ahead of her, as they ran for their lives.

She was beyond feeling cold or warmth, beyond feeling anything but the pain scraping through her ribs, her lungs, and most of all her hand. She looked down briefly and saw scarlet striping her palm, more red in the melting snow, like a spray of poppies. Her head spun.

Oskar was speaking to her, saying words that were as incomprehensible as wind, as soothing as warm water. Papa dropped back to run beside her with Sanna and

Geir, Pípa on his back. She looked into his face, his blue eyes wide with concern. Behind them was the column of smoke that was swallowing the Bear's tree. She thought she saw something vast and dark moving toward them. Something running.

She faded in and out of the world as she ran, at times blinded by black, at others by light, riding the swell and fall, the red edge of pain that ate up her arm, through to her bones, formed a fog around her brain. *It's like cold*, she thought. Like being caught out in a snowstorm, or buried in that snow crush. The pain was so entire it was all there was, spreading out to the very edges of her being.

"Mila, you saved me," Oskar said, like a prayer, or a wish. "Mila. Mila, don't stop now."

But she could not help it—the pain was too great. She stumbled.

"I can't carry her across there," she heard him say. "We need to spread out."

"There's no time!" came Geir's panicked voice.

Mila forced her heavy lids open as she felt Oskar brace his arm under her, taking her weight. They stood at the island's edge, and ahead, blue-white and broad as the sky, stretched the frozen sea. Boys were already running recklessly onto the ice.

But the sea would not stay frozen. Web lines of bubbles were rushing through the cracks, hair-thin for now, but quickly releasing in the sunlight, pushing out. She thought she could almost hear the sea breathing, sighing as it stretched its caught body, finally flexing free of winter's grip.

"Why won't it stop bleeding?" said Pípa's voice beside her.

Fluttering in the corner of her vision were anxious hands and pale faces, and she looked down dully. Pípa and Sanna were moving her arm, but she could not believe it was her hand they touched, looking for the best point to bind it. She could barely believe that thing was a hand. It was purple and black and red as a thunderstorm viewed through closed lids, the white bone flashing through like lightning—

No.

She looked away. It was better to keep her balance, keep her grip. She leaned into her father. Her papa. *Alive.*

He was solid beneath her arms, his breath steady and strong. He was here. He was real, he was really real . . .

. . . but she could feel herself fading, becoming less, blood seeming to drain the wrong way, drain upward, away from her legs . . .

She frowned and looked down. Her legs did look less there. And they felt less there too, numbing as though submerged in a snowdrift. It seemed that, without the sea's winter ice to keep it in place, Thule was melting from their realm. With a bolt of clarity, she realized that they would vanish with it.

"Go," she whispered.

"Mila, did you say something?" Oskar brought his head to her face and she spoke again into his ear.

"Thule is going. We need to go."

Oskar looked down too, and yelped. Completely ignoring Papa, he threw Mila's uninjured arm over his shoulders and helped her stand.

"Get Pípa—we need to run!" They stepped onto the ice, and when it did not creak, they picked up their pace, moving in steady, low strides, almost skating. Mila looked back and saw Papa lift Pípa.

Cries from the other boys went up like gulls as the ice groaned under the weight of so many people. Thule was disappearing in great swallows. The white ice was as thin as cloth worn by washing, the remaining patches pegged out at intervals along the island's disappearing edge.

Mila heard a purring like a giant cat, and a clack of claws as ice splintered further. She saw the ocean exhaling a stream of bubbles under ice now glass-thin. It was melting as fast as Thule was fading.

And coming ever closer behind them, there was a man, gold cord still binding his ankles, gold eyes fixed on Mila's face.

The Bear was still alive, and he was coming for her.

"Nearly there," panted Oskar, as much to himself as to Mila. "I can see Bovnik."

But they were not going to make it in time. Even if the Bear did not reach them, even if the ice held a little longer, Oskar was tiring. Mila could see Papa and Pípa wavering too, already overtaken by some of the boys. None of them were stopping to help, not with solid land so nearby. She took her weight from Oskar's shoulders.

"Go ahead."

"What?"

"You go on ahead. He's coming for me."

Oskar looked back and yelped, clutching her hand, pulling her on quicker and quicker. But it was not enough.

"It's me he wants," Mila cried. "Go!"

"I'll go nowhere without you, Milenka," he replied.

Mila wrenched her hand from his grip. But even as she freed herself, Oskar stumbled. He was weak, and she knew he would not make it to the shore without her help. She set her jaw, and in mimicry of his earlier action, placed his arm around her shoulders. She barely had the strength to remain upright, but she looked away from the Bear's awful shape and back toward Bovnik, eyes filling with tears. A shadow was moving toward them across the ice, like a beetle scuttling from the shore. More joined it, becoming a swarm.

She blinked the blur away hurriedly and a shout went up from one of the boys running alongside them.

"Sleighs!"

Mila blinked again and saw that there were dogs pulling sleigh after sleigh over the thick ice closest to shore. The inhabitants of Bovnik were coming to the boys' aid. One sleigh was moving faster than all the others, and before it drew close enough for Mila to see the driver's face, she knew.

"Rune!"

The ice cracked thunder beneath them. Mila heard the familiar warning barks of Dusha and Danya as she practically threw Oskar into the bed of the sleigh before collapsing beside him.

Mila willed herself to stay conscious, feeling Rune's hand squeeze her shoulder gently as Pípa and Sanna leapt into the sleigh, Papa and Geir collapsing on top of them, their bodies a tangle of limbs.

"Sanna, take the reins!" shouted Rune.

But still, the Bear was coming. She knew he would not stop until he caught them.

"Rune, he's—"

"I know."

She cracked open her eyelids to see the mage's strange, kind face up close, his moonstone eyes fixed on hers.

"You did it, Mila. Which means it's time for me to go."

"What do you—?"

"You lured him off Thule." Rune reached out and tenderly tucked a strand of hair behind her ear. "Do you understand? Now I can put things right."

"Put things—" Pain was making everything hazy.

"It could only be now, Mila. The forest needs a guardian, and it's found a new one. You're the guardian of the forest now, Mila." His cool hand squeezed hers. "Take care of it."

"Me?" Mila's head swam.

"Look after Lunka for me," he said.

"Rune? You're scaring me. Where are you going?"

"To the Bear."

She gripped him desperately, but he pulled gently away from her grasp. "This was always what had to happen, Mila. I was always the one who had to do it."

"Do what?"

"This."

And then he was gone. Mila forced herself upright, watching Rune's slight shape run as fast as wind toward the Bear.

"What is he doing?" shouted Sanna.

"He must have eaten all the flameberry!" cried Pípa.

"*Farash!*" yelled Oskar.

Mila felt a wrenching in her stomach as they set off. The dogs flew. Thule was wholly faded from their realm now, and the ice was breaking up and floating to fill the space it had left.

Rune and the Bear met with a crashing force that seemed to set the air shimmering around them. Surely Rune was no match for the Bear?

"Don't look, Milenka," said Papa. He maneuvered himself alongside her and wrapped his arm around her. But she kept her eyes on Rune and saw the mage throw a glitter of black powder at the Bear's feet. There was a flash of brimstone, a crack, and they both disappeared beneath the ice.

"No!" Mila tried to throw herself toward Rune, but she was held fast by Papa and Sanna and Pípa. She raged and cried, looking back desperately, but the ice continued to break up around them. No one emerged from the sea.

"Farash!" cried Oskar again, and the dogs seemed to run even faster just as there was another bone-shuddering *crunch.*

Two shadows rose over the ice. Mila gaped. Even at this distance she could see that one was a massive bear, and the other some sort of bird.

"A gyrfalcon!" Pípa cried. "Mila, it's Rune's gyrfalcon!"

As they watched, two more gyrfalcons joined him. They formed a shimmering barrier between the Bear and the mainland, their mighty wings transparent and linked. Mila's heart swelled. Rune's mother and grand-mother, the great mages of old, had come to face the Bear with Rune.

Mila expected them to fight, the spirits of the Bear and Rune and his family, but instead they hovered, facing each other over the unlocking sea.

"What are they doing?" said Sanna, muffled beneath her sisters. "Why doesn't he attack?"

The gyrfalcons began to circle gently, the Bear floating, his mighty shoulders heaving. Finally Rune-as-gyrfalcon brushed the Bear's shoulder with his wing, and the Bear turned toward the faded Thule. Despite herself, some of the ache in her chest was for him, watching as he followed his burning forest into nothing. The shape of him faded, and then he was gone.

The horizon flickered as Thule and the Bear van-ished into another realm, then settled. Rune's spirit lifted on the air, circling higher and higher into the blue, until Mila could not see it for brightness and tears.

Sanna shimmied down to lie on Mila's other side, and hugged her tightly. Then there was a pressing weight on top, as Pípa stretched out over them all. There was a bump, and the sound of the sleigh changed from smooth ice running to a clogged, deep-snow hush.

"*Stuta*," said Oskar, in a voice thick with tears.

The dogs stopped and Mila heard them panting, heard the soft *putt* of their bodies collapse in the snow. Another shift of weight rolled them all sideways as Oskar lay down, lacing his fingers through the web of arms so he touched each of them.

The sound of her family's breathing filled Mila's ears, and she let herself fade, like Thule, like Rune and the Bear, into nothingness.

CHAPTER THIRTY-ONE

Name-Giving

*M*ila lay on a cloud, warm sun on her face. Her body felt far away and light as air. A hand, cool and dry as paper, settled into hers, and someone spoke her name. *Rune?*

She opened her eyes. The sun turned into tickling fingers of fire, the cloud a straw mattress beneath her. And a face, familiar but aged, beamed down at her.

"Welcome back," said Papa.

"She's awake?" There was a scrambling, and someone knelt painfully on her hair. Pípa hovered over her, eyebrows knotted and anxious. "She's awake!"

"Not so loud, Pípa," chided Oskar, easing her off Mila's hair. Pípa stayed bent over her, breath tickling Mila's nose. She seemed to want to fix her sister's face in her mind, to be sure she would not disappear again.

Mila blinked. She was in a small, light room. The walls were stone, their outer edges curved, and she realized she must be in one of the houses in Bovnik.

"My hand," Mila said, voice coming raw through her throat.

"It'll be sore for a while, and you'll have a wicked scar." Oskar held up his own hand, with the jagged line left by her crooked stitches from when she'd sewn it after the sleigh runners had cut it open, an age ago. "We'll match."

"Where . . . ?"

"Bovnik," said Sanna, coming to kneel at Mila's other side. "Rune saved us. He gathered the remaining people of Bovnik, and when he saw the ice melting, he led the sleighs to us."

"I remember," said Mila, the ice-crossing coming back to her. "He . . . he killed the Bear."

Sanna nodded, placing a gentle hand on her arm. Mila fell back into her body at Sanna's touch. The sadness spun through Mila, sucking at her like a whirlpool.

"He sacrificed himself. He's a hero."

"You all are," said Papa. His voice was warm and wonderful. She looked up at him, his blue eyes, his broad face, stretched wider in a smile that made her heart ache.

"What happened, Papa?" Mila's instinct was to reach out to him, but she kept her hand still, and his broad fingers twitched. He was wearing his garnet ring again. She was remembering now, remembering the Bear's story. Remembering that Papa had killed the heart-tree. She turned a furious gaze upon him. She had to hear it from him. "What did you do?"

His face creased, and a stifled sob caught in his throat. Oskar placed a steadying hand on his shoulders. "I'm so sorry," he whispered. "I never meant to—"

"Tell her, Papa," said Sanna.

Papa could not look Mila in the eye. He fixed his gaze at her chin. "The day I left. I never meant to go for good. I missed your mama." He stopped, chest heaving, taking deep breaths. "I missed her so badly. I was angry with her for going, at the forest for not protecting her. And that story she always told, I was angry at that, too. I thought it could not be true, because she loved the forest, and still it did not keep her alive. I wanted . . ." He looked up at Mila. "I wanted to hurt—something. So I walked. I walked for miles and miles, and suddenly I was at the heart-tree. . . ." He broke off. "I couldn't see for anger. I just lifted my axe and starting swinging."

Fresh tears came to Mila's eyes, rage hot inside her. "But the heart-tree. It was sacred, Papa."

He hung his head. "What I did was unforgivable. When he came, I hardly fought. I left my ring like it was nothing, gave up my axe. I deserved what I got."

A part of Mila agreed, roared with anger at his stupidity, his selfishness. She remembered Rune telling her that she and the Bear were alike in some ways, and she supposed this was one.

"How did you know it was Papa in the tree?" Oskar was frowning at her. "How did you know the Bear had taken him?"

"The Bear told us," said Mila. She felt suddenly exhausted, though she had just woken from a deep sleep. "He said that, five years ago, a man had tried to cut down his heart-tree, so in revenge he took a cutting of the tree to Thule, and planted the man as its heart." She shuddered, remembering her father's wooden body. "And his axe, I knew it." She glanced at Papa. "It was yours."

"Forgive me, Milenka. All of you." Papa's face was wretched. "I never meant to cause such harm."

"But you did," she said, and she felt the sadness seize her from within. "There is no undoing the harm you did."

Papa met her gaze. "I know," he whispered. "I would do anything to put it right."

These words stirred a memory inside her. Rune, atop the trading platform, had wanted to put his wrongs right. And he had, as best he could. Her heart was sore, thinking of the destroyed heart-tree, the forest caught for so long in a slow, wintry death. But Eldbjørn Forest had survived, and now spring was returning. And she could not live as the Bear had, with anger in her heart. Rune had told her her purpose. She was the guardian of the forest now, and would not let it, or its people, down.

"We'll need to plant a new heart-tree," said Mila decisively. "And take better care of it from now on. No more chopping things down without planting first. No more building, until the forest heals."

"Of course," said Papa, his wrinkled face creased with regret and relief.

"We all will," said Oskar. "The boys will do anything you say. And their families arrived from Stavgar two days ago. We can spread the word."

"We've been feasting every day," said Pípa excitedly. "I've had candied plums three times already."

"It's a wonderful place," said Sanna. "There are so many beautiful things here."

Oskar reached across and put a hand on Sanna's, and Mila caught a look passing between them, as though Oskar was stopping Sanna from saying more. Pípa gabbled on.

"They're calling us the spring sisters because we burned down the tree and freed the spring." She snorted. "Geir came up with it. That's clever, don't you think, Sanna?"

Sanna blushed and looked down.

"That's enough," said Papa, semi-sternly. "Do I have to rethink my promise, Pípa?"

"What promise?" said Mila.

"Papa said that when you were awake, I could have my given name."

"But she's not yet eight!" said Mila, surprised.

"She has proven herself ready," said Papa. "I think it is time."

Pípa looked expectantly at their father, who cleared his throat and placed his hand on her shoulder. Mila remembered him adopting this pose for her on her eighth birthday, the weight of his touch, the lightness that spread through her when she heard her true name.

"Your name," he said solemnly, as Pípa rocked on her heels with excitement. "Is Agneta."

There was a pause. Pípa wrinkled her nose. "I don't like it."

"It was Mama's name," huffed Sanna.

"Well, then, she shouldn't have to share," said Pípa, and Oskar stifled a laugh. "Can I pick another?"

Papa looked as if he were about to protest, but his face quickly softened with amusement. "I suppose a spring sister should be allowed at least that."

"Rune," said Pípa without hesitation. "I'll have Agneta as my middle name," she added hurriedly to Papa. "But my name, if you don't mind, is Rune."

Papa let out a long exhale. He reached out and brushed a stray hair from Pípa's face. Watching him, Mila felt a warmth grow inside her, a happy sadness so strong it made her insides feel raw. She could forgive him, she decided. She could help the forest heal.

"All right," Papa said finally. "Rune-Agneta Orekson. All right."

CHAPTER THIRTY-TWO

Home

Mila ate so many candied plums that she was sure sugar was running through her veins in place of blood the next day. The inhabitants of Bovnik had already begun to return in the time she had been unconscious, and it had been a magnificent feast.

Bovnik's meethouse was carved out of the mountainside, and was five times larger than Stavgar's. On the walls were carved the names of all the families of Bovnik, and they found Mama's beneath her parents'. Oskar used his knife to write their father's name beside it, drawing a line between their parents' names and then another vertical line down. Beneath this he wrote his and his sisters' names, so it read:

Agneta — Yelfer

|

Sanna * *Oskar* * *Mila* * *Rune-Agneta*

When he was done it looked like a tree with very strong roots.

The room was filled with furs and wine and merriment, but Mila did not want to be around so many people. She missed the mage so much it was like a permanent headache that made everything too loud, too bright.

She, Oskar, and Rune-Agneta sneaked away early, their pockets full of sugared fruit, climbed up to the trading platform, and ate them overlooking the waterfall, thawed now and rushing toward the unfrozen and endless sea. Sanna had stayed at the feast, laughing and dancing with Geir while Papa looked on sternly.

———≫≫≫·—

A small procession of sleighs stood loaded and ready to take them to Stavgar, and then on to home. Dusha and Danya were well rested, the spring routes would be nearly thawed, and in such a large group the danger from wolves would be less. Mila felt a thrill at the thought that she would soon be home. And things would be even better than before, because Papa was returning with them.

She piled onto the bed of the sleigh with her little sister.

"Look," Rune-Agneta whispered, showing Mila her pockets. They were stuffed full of candied plums. Mila shook her head as Oskar came out of the kennel with some extra food for the dogs.

"Where is that girl?" said Papa impatiently. "They'll set off without us if we're not careful."

"Here she comes," said Oskar, pointing, and Mila saw Sanna's elegant figure descending the stone ladder ahead. Oskar came to stand beside the sleigh and gently stroked both his sisters' hair, comforting them.

Mila looked sharply up at him. "What's wrong?"

But he only shook his head, and Mila felt a rising sense of unease as Sanna approached. She was wearing Geir's brooch, newly fixed, and was chewing her lip.

"Where's your bag?" said Papa. "We have to leave."

"I . . ." Sanna's voice caught in her throat, and she looked at Oskar, almost pleadingly. Mila understood.

"You're not coming," she said.

Sanna, eyes glassy, opened her mouth and closed it again. She shook her head.

"What do you mean, not coming?" said Rune-Agneta.

"I—I'm staying here," said Sanna. "I'm going to stay here, with Geir."

"But you have to come home. We came all this way."

Tears spilled down Mila's cheeks. She felt as if she were back on Thule, all color fading again as she looked into her sister's beautiful face.

"Exactly. We came all this way. And I want to keep going. The world is so big and I want to see it. You know I do, Milenka. And Geir"—Sanna's cheeks flushed crimson but she didn't stop talking—"he wants to see it too. We're going to pass a spring here, and then in summer we'll go south."

She looked at Papa, whose face was still, as though he were a tree again. She kept talking, faster and faster. "We'll come past home, see you all. Maybe . . . maybe we'll race winter so that it won't ever reach us again." She drew a shaky breath.

None of them spoke, only stared at her. Oskar was still stroking Mila's hair, and she realized that he had known this was coming. She felt a flush of anger.

"How can you do this?" she burst out. "How can you leave us, after all we've gone through to get home—?"

"No, Mila," said Oskar gently. "You came to get me."

"Yes, but now we have to go home," said Mila desperately. "Now things have to go on as they were!"

Oskar shook his head, smiling sadly. "Things can't always stay the same, Milenka."

"You always wanted to leave us," said Mila bitterly to Sanna.

"It's not about leaving you," said Sanna, striding quickly to the sleigh and holding out her arms to Mila. "I love you. I love all of you." She turned to Rune-Agneta, then to Oskar, and finally to Papa. "Seeing you again is beyond anything I hoped for."

She reached out her hand to Papa, and he took it, pulling her close. She still fit beneath his chin. They stood like that for a long moment, before Sanna drew gently away and raised her face to his.

"I want to cross oceans, Papa. I want to have adventures. None so dangerous as this one, though." She laughed weakly, then caught sight of Mila's face. Mila knew she must look murderous. "My Milenka . . . if you don't want me to go—" She swallowed. "I won't."

A bitter twist of spite went through Mila. She could tell her sister not to go, could keep Sanna with them, keep everything as it once was. But Mila saw how

Sanna's face shone at the thought of the journey. She thought of how she felt now, so far from the forest, as if her heart could not settle. If that was how Sanna felt when she was stuck in one place, Mila could not say anything to change her mind.

"Be happy," Mila said, voice cracking. "You have to promise to be happy."

Sanna pulled her tightly to her. "I will."

"Will you come and see us?" said Rune-Agneta, crying openly now.

"As much as I can," said Sanna. "And I will carry you with me, all of you. The way you feel about the forest, Milenka, I felt that too, for a while. And now I think I could feel that about Bovnik. And when I stop feeling it about here, I'll go somewhere else. I'll have hundreds of homes, maybe. But wherever you are, wherever Píp—I mean Rune—is, or Oskar, or Papa, that is my true home."

"*Farash!*" The first sleigh started to peel away, through the gates and around the edge of the mountain.

"I love you," said Mila, throwing her arms around her big sister's neck, breathing her in.

"Always," said Sanna, hugging her back, and Oskar, Rune-Agneta and Papa joined the bundle. They heard sleigh after sleigh set off; finally, it was their turn. Mila did not want to let go. She looked into Sanna's face, and her sister leaned down and pressed a kiss onto her forehead.

"Go safe, go sound."

Papa held her close before jerking the reins. Mila twisted to watch Sanna raise her hand, and disappear from view.

Mila hugged her little sister close as Oskar stood at the front of the sleigh with Papa, arms around each other's shoulders. She felt the wind in her face, breathed in the air, which had already lost its chill. Overhead, a shadow swirled. She narrowed her eyes and squinted. A gyrfalcon wheeled high above them, pale as moonstone.

A lifting in Mila's chest matched its wind-winging. Soon they would be home, and for the first time in years the green shoots would be raising their arms above the ground, the trees unfurling their leaves and tipping them up to the sun. They would plant a new heart-tree, and grow the forest strong—stronger even than the Bear had done.

Soon they would be home, bringing spring.

Acknowledgments

First thanks always to my family. To my mother, who reads every draft and answers every panicked phone call. To my father, who shows me the wild edges of the world and tells me to keep writing into them. To my brother, for whom I wrote this book, because he is brave in all things, especially in forging his own path. Be safe on your adventures. To my grandfather and grandmother—I adore you with my whole heart. To O, and L, and most of all, N.

To all the Millwoods, Hargraves, Karers, Kakkars, Slomans, de Frestons, Cautherys, Furnivalls, and Joneses around the world. Especially to my precious Sabine, and the gorgeous Tilly, Fred, Emily, Isla, Pippa, and Teddy. It is such a blessing to have you all in my lives, showing me daily what marvels kids are.

To my friends, who strike the perfect balance between guiding me and leading me astray, and especially to Daisy Johnson, Sarvat Hasin, Katie Webber, Anna James, Kate Rundell, Kevin Tsang, M.G. Leonard, Maz Evans, Melinda Salisbury, Cat Doyle, James Nicol, Lucy Strange, Frances Hardinge, Lucy Ayrton, Laura Theis, Sam Guglani, Samantha Shannon, Abi Elphinstone, and the Unruly Writers. Thank you to Fiona Noble for your support and kindness.

Thank you to the Janklow & Nesbit team, and to Hellie Ogden and Kirby Kim, my agents and friends. You are both fierce and wonderful, and I'm so glad you're on my side.

Thank you to my team at Chicken House, especially my editor Rachel. Thank you to all at Chronicle, especially Taylor Norman, whose unerring passion and understanding for this book have helped me grow it into what it always wanted to be. I am so grateful to have you as my editor, and excited for what we have made to go out into the world.

Thank you to all the readers who want to come on these adventures with me.

Last thanks always to my husband, Tom. Thank you for the pep talks, the reading aloud, the constant inspiration, and the endless, endless love. What a tremendous thing it is, to get to share my life with you.